Owl-Light

Maggie Pearson lives in a sixteenth–century cottage in Suffolk. She has worked as a librarian, barmaid, au pair, corn-dolly maker and freelance journalist, but mostly as a mother. Now that her three sons are grown–up, she is a full–time writer.

Owl-Light

Maggie Pearson

Hodder
Children's
Books

a division of Hodder Headline plc

PC0332

With thanks to Tim for the picture, Mike for the bananas and Jerry for mowing the lawn while I was busy writing.

One

A werewolf is nothing to be afraid of. Gran said so, so it must be right.

'Once upon a time,' said Gran, 'but not so very long ago either, for the world was already nearly as old then as it is now – once upon a time, there was an animal called Man. He lived in a cave and he ate mostly roots and berries. But sometimes he hunted the other animals, and sometimes the other animals hunted him.

'And, true to his animal nature, he was alive to every sound and scent and shadow in the world about him.

'But Man grew to be a whole lot cleverer than any animal that had gone before. In no more than a million years or so – which is no time at all, if we're talking about the history of the world – Man had worked out how to make things like aeroplanes and television and digital watches.

'And somewhere along the way, as people do who've suddenly gone up in the world, he began to be ashamed of his poor relations, the animals.

'Most of all, he was ashamed of that small part of himself which still heard the call of the wild, lonely places and whose dream would always be to hunt the badger by owl-light and run with the deer and to live in tune with the changing of the seasons.

'Man was ashamed – and a little afraid. And so he made up stories to frighten himself about a creature that could not resist the call. A creature that was half-man, half-wolf.

'He called this creature the werewolf.'

It was a Saturday afternoon and as usual the three of them were in Gran's kitchen: Gran and Ellie and Hal.

Four of them, if you counted Uncle Ho, the cat. He was lying in the sunlight just inside the porch, watching the butterflies drinking themselves tiddly on the flowers of honesty and sweet rocket just outside.

Hal was curled up in the big armchair, with a book

that used to be Dad's, knowing he could sit there all afternoon if he wanted, and no one would ask him if he couldn't find something better to do.

Gran stood at the big, square table, making bread. She'd given a bit of the dough to Ellie, who was pummelling it into some sort of animal shape.

'What's that you're making, Ellie?' asked Gran.

'A wolf,' said Ellie.

Trust Ellie, thought Hal. Other girls her age would have settled for a pastry-man or a nice pussy-cat.

'A werewolf,' she said, dragging out the snout until it looked as if it had been crossed with an elephant. She picked up a cocktail stick and began marking in the teeth. 'A werewolf, with eyes like fire and teeth dripping blood, coming to get you in the dark! Grrrrah!'

Hal shuddered. He was afraid of the dark.

Gran glanced at him, just briefly. 'Silly Ellie!' she said gently. 'A werewolf is nothing to be afraid of.' Then she explained, about Man and his animal relations. Quietly she talked, her strong fingers squeezing and kneading the dough. 'You're not afraid of Uncle Ho, are you? He goes wandering in the dark, not just once in a while, but every night.

And he doesn't become some fearsome monster, he just becomes more himself.'

But Ellie was under the table, grubbing for the currants she was using to make the wolf's eyes. 'I'm going to be a werewolf,' she announced, bobbing up again.

'You can't,' said Hal. 'You weren't listening. Gran said a werewolf is half-man, half-wolf. You're a girl.'

It took Ellie less than five seconds to sweep that obstacle out of the way. 'That was in the olden days,' she said. 'Girls can be anything they want now, can't they, Gran?'

Gran had to agree that women could be doctors or lawyers or even prime ministers if they set their minds to it.

'Or lorry drivers or car mechanics,' added Ellie.

Hal could see Gran looking a bit doubtful about that: she could probably just about imagine Ellie being elected Prime Minister, but she couldn't see anyone in their right mind letting her loose with a spanner under the bonnet of their car.

'I think,' said Gran, 'that werewolves would probably have to be born that way, not made. That's not to say there isn't a bit of the wolf nature in all of

10

us. It's the bit that tells you blackberries taste best picked and eaten straight from the hedge; the bit that makes you want to stamp in puddles and scuff up the autumn leaves; the bit that makes strangers smile at one another in the street on the first warm day of spring.'

Later, when they got home and Hal started telling Mum what Gran had said on the subject of werewolves, Ellie kicked him hard on the ankle and started on about what *fun* they'd had, helping Gran make *lovely* home-baked bread.

It was hard to believe this was the same Ellie who'd been up to her elbows in pond water only an hour before, trying to do a head count of the tadpoles. ('They've been doing it again!' she said crossly. 'Eating each other.') Who, when Gran rang the bell to let them know that tea was ready, came crawling out of the undergrowth on the edge of the common with burrs in her hair and her knees plastered with mud.

'You know we're not supposed to go on the common,' he scolded her.

Mum had taken one look at the common on the day they moved in and promptly put it out of bounds. 'You never know who you might meet there,' she said.

Hal couldn't imagine meeting anyone worse than the Stittles and he was bound to run into them at school. But if Mum said the common was out of bounds, that was that.

Not so Ellie. 'I was only on the edge,' she said. 'Besides, Mum won't know unless you tell her, will she?'

Now she was Little Miss Frilly Knickers, chattering on, while Mum smiled and nodded, though she wasn't really listening. Most of her attention was taken up with trying to shovel some food into Jack, which was a lot harder to do than it sounds, since Jack had changed from a toddling waste-disposal unit into a banana-diet freak.

'That's good,' said Dad. 'He'll be cheap to feed.'

'Just lay in a good stock of bananas,' was Gran's advice. 'He'll soon get bored.'

But Mum said Jack had got to learn that life wasn't just about having your own way. He'd got to learn who was boss. It seemed to Hal that Jack didn't need to learn who was boss. He knew already. He was.

Every day, three times a day, he had Mum at his mercy, begging, threatening, scolding, pleading with him to take just one spoonful of something that wasn't banana.

Ellie took the bread-wolf out of her bag and laid it on the tray of the high chair.

'That's nice,' said Mum. 'Look, Jack. A tortoise.' It had spread a bit in the cooking, but Hal didn't think it was that bad.

Jack picked it up and inspected it. 'Nana?' he suggested, as if to say, if I eat this, *then* do I get a banana?

'Rather you than me, Jack,' muttered Hal, remembering Ellie's sticky fingers grubbing about on the kitchen floor.

'No banana,' Mum said firmly. 'Nice scrambled egg.'

Jack puffed up his cheeks and batted the spoon away.

Hal started explaining that it wasn't a tortoise: it was a wolf. And he was telling her again what Gran had said, when Ellie butted in, with how the tadpoles in Gran's pond had *grown*, but that there weren't so many as last week, because they would keep *eating* each other, ugh!

Hal gave up and wandered into the living-room to fetch himself a banana. Jack was furious when he saw it. He turned bright red and started trying to climb out of his high chair.

'Oh, Hal!' said Mum.

'You know what happens when you eat too many bananas?' said Hal to Jack. 'You turn into a monkey.' He started doing his monkey impression round the kitchen, knees bent, scratching himself under his arms, until Jack forgot to be cross and began to laugh.

His little mouth opened wide. Mum lunged with the spoon – but she wasn't quite quick enough, which was just as well, because Jack's jaws snapped shut so fast, he'd have bitten the bowl clean off if she'd got the spoon inside.

'You've got egg on your blouse, Mum,' said Hal.

'What? Oh, sugar! Ellie, hold this.' She gave Ellie the bowl of egg and the spoon, rushed over to the sink, turned on the tap and began rubbing washing-up liquid on to her blouse.

Hal bit the top off his banana and popped it into Jack's mouth. When Mum turned round, she saw him happily chomping away at something yellow.

'Oh, Ellie!' she said. 'You are clever!'

Jack opened his mouth to show her the banana and Ellie shoved in a spoonful of scrambled egg.

Jack chewed away happily on egg and banana mixed.

'Now,' said Mum, taking back the bowl. 'One more for Mummy!' But Jack's mouth stayed firmly shut. 'Never mind,' said Mum. 'I think we're winning. Give him his banana, Ellie, while I tidy up.'

Hal wandered into the living-room and switched on the telly. After a while Ellie came in, picked up the remote control and began stabbing furiously at the buttons.

'Peabrain!' she muttered. 'Bonehead! Button fluff!' Ellie collected insults. She knew more than anyone in her class.

'What did I do?' said Hal. 'What did I say?'

'Telling Mum all that stuff! "Gran says we're all werewolves underneath." Honestly!'

'I thought it was interesting.'

'You know what Mum thinks about Gran.' And without giving Hal time to say whether he did or not, she ploughed on: 'She thinks Gran's going daft, doolally, bonkers, losing her marbles —'

'She's not.'

'I know she's not. You know she's not.'

'Why does Mum think she is, then?'

'Things she says. Things she does. She doesn't always know what time it is. Or even what day.'

'Codswallop,' he said. 'If you can't do what you want when you want when you're as old as Gran . . .'

'She'll stop us going there,' Ellie said. 'So just watch what you say. OK?'

Hal left her sitting cross-legged on the settee, glaring at the football results. He didn't tell her the programme she wanted to watch was starting on another channel.

Saturday afternoons at Gran's had turned out to be the best thing about moving to Laxworth. Sometimes it seemed to Hal it was the only good thing about the whole business. He missed his friends and he missed the town, the distant hum of activity day and night and the streetlamp outside his window, a small oasis of light in the darkness.

When Mum had Jack there wasn't room for them all in the flat. It seemed like a good idea to buy a house near Gran. 'She's not getting any younger,' said Mum to Dad. 'She'll be glad to have us living near. She'll see more of Hal and Ellie. Perhaps, if she could have Jack during the day, I could get a part-time job. It'll be good for all of us. Living in the country.'

Dad said, 'I thought you didn't like the country.'

Mum said, 'Everyone likes the country.'

It was only after they'd moved there that she realised she hated the country. She hated the huge spiders that invaded the house in warm, damp weather. She hated being miles from the shops. She hated the common which seemed to creep nearer to the back of the house every time she looked. And no way was she going to leave Jack with Gran. Gran had turned out to be a big disappointment.

A gran was supposed to be a little old lady in a sensible skirt and twinset and pearls, quietly knitting by the fire. If their gran decided to do a bit of knitting, the first thing she did was get on her bike and cycle off to see old Mr Stittle, to ask him if he could get her a fleece. Old Mr Stittle would chew on his gums (because he never put his teeth in, except for meals) and say he'd ask about. And a few days later he would turn up at Gran's with the fleece on the back seat of his Mini.

Then Gran would get out her spinning-wheel and the kitchen would be filled with its gentle murmur, hour after hour, day after day. Soon she'd be off out again, looking for stuff to dye the wool with: heather from the common; leaves and lichens from the wood; berries and nettles; geraniums and onion skins. Things people used for dyes in the olden days, giving soft shades of brown and yellow and grey and green and pinky-beige. Finally she'd get down to the knitting, making up the pattern as she went along.

Some people might say that was a lot of trouble to go to, when she could have strolled down to the wool shop for a few hundred grams of double knit. But, Gran would say, she'd had weeks of fun – and exercise – all for the two bottles of elderberry wine and the bagful of apples that old Mr Stittle took home with him in his Mini.

There were people who said Mr Stittle ought not to be allowed out in that Mini. Newcomers to the village. The rest knew he never went more than five miles from home; never drove at more than twenty miles an hour; and sounded his horn every hundred metres so there was plenty of time to get out of the way.

Even Mr Harding-Froggett in his Porsche used to get off the road when he heard old Mr Stittle coming, because Mr Stittle had a right to use that road, more than anyone else in Laxworth. There had been Stittles living in Laxworth since before the Norman Conquest.

Some people grow to look like their dogs. The Stittles had grown to look like the oldest houses in the village: squat and pale, with a bit of ragged thatch on top.

Hal had been warned about them on his first day at the new school.

Dad said, 'I'm sure they're not that bad. Try and be friends with them.'

He had tried. But after he'd been knocked down and sat on by three different Stittles (the last time by Madonna Stittle, who was only five) he decided they didn't want to be friends. They wanted him to hate them, like everyone else did.

Hal lay on his bed, reading the book he'd brought back from Gran's. He heard Mum carrying Jack upstairs, softly singing 'The Skye Boat Song'. He heard Dad come in from photographing the ladies of the WI among the rhododendrons. Dad went out again almost at once, bound for the May Ball at the Further Education College, leaving early, so as to meet up first with Frank Finnegan, ace reporter for the *Melford Mercury*.

They worked together a lot, Dad and Frank Finnegan. Fêtes and flower shows, mostly. Golden weddings, supermarket openings and Masonic dinners. But once or twice a month the phone would ring and it would be Frank. 'Drop what you're doing, Dan, and get yourself down here. I need some pictures *now*!' It was always a fire or a car crash or a demo that had suddenly turned ugly. If the *Melford Mercury* couldn't use them, there was a good chance of getting in first with the London papers.

Hal heard Ellie coming up the stairs. He got up, undressed, climbed back into bed and went on reading.

Outside, next-door's cat was howling to be let in. Unlike Uncle Ho, it was afraid of the dark. Sometimes Hal wondered if it actually knew it was a cat at all. He'd seen it through the window, watching *Neighbours* all by itself.

Then suddenly it was dark, except for the moonlight streaming in between the curtains. He must have been asleep for hours. Even before he was properly awake, he knew there was something wrong. Not wrong. Missing.

Ellie.

When they were younger and lived in the flat, Ellie used to share his room. Waking in the night, he'd hear her breathing. If she was awake, he'd know it straight away and check to see what she wanted: a drink of water; a trip to the loo; a cuddle, because she'd had a bad dream. Mum used to say, 'Ellie's such a good baby. She never wakes.'

Ever since they'd had separate rooms, if he woke in the night he could still sense her there, just the other side of the wall. But not tonight.

He got up and went to the door. By the moonlight on the landing he could see the bathroom door wide open. No Ellie. No sounds from downstairs. No light. He pushed open Ellie's bedroom door. The bed was empty, moonlight spread over it. The curtains billowed gently in the draught from the open window.

Open? Yes. Then pushed to from the outside, otherwise she would have used the catch. Hal opened the window wide and called, quietly, so as not to wake Mum and Dad, 'Ellie?'

The roof of the utility room jutted out just below. From there it was only a step down to the coal bunker, then to the ground. He'd climbed in and out that way lots of times when they first moved in. Ellie had always needed help, but she'd grown since then.

He glanced over Ellie's worldly goods, scattered across the bedroom floor. Clothes, cuddly toys, Lego, some interesting rocks . . . He spotted the sweater she'd worn that day, but not her jeans or trainers. Of course, she'd got other sweaters. He turned back to the window.

Clouds were scudding across the full moon. The wind sighed in the treetops, but at ground level everything was still. Not a leaf, not a blade of grass stirred the whole length of the garden. Beyond the chain-link fence, far out across the common, as far as he could see, the world was trapped in moonlight, like flies in the chunk of amber that Gran's sister, Aunt May, had brought back from Poland.

Trapped for a million years.

He heard a car on the bypass. As the sound faded, he had the weirdest feeling that he, not the car, was travelling away. Tumbling backwards through time, until he was afraid to turn his head, in case the houses either side were gone and there was nothing there but the wild, lonely places Gran spoke of when she told them about the werewolf.

Somewhere a dog howled.

Hal clung to the window-ledge – slowly reassured by the painted wood under his fingers – waiting for the giddiness to pass. Then he eased his way backwards until the edge of the bed caught him behind the knees and he suddenly sat down. He decided to wait there until Ellie came back. She might need help getting in. And then he could ask her . . . ask her . . .

'What are you doing in my bed?' demanded Ellie.

'Huh?' said Hal. 'Where did you go?'

'I asked first. What are you doing in my bed?'

'Waiting for you. Where did you go?'

'Nowhere. I'm here.'

'You weren't here. In the middle of the night.' His brain was still muzzy with sleep, still half in a dream in which Ellie, with a little furry face and pointy ears, padded four-footed through the dark. 'I came in and you weren't here.'

'I went to get a drink of water.'

'In the dark?'

'There was moonlight. Go away now. I want to get dressed.'

Her jeans were lying in the middle of the floor. He couldn't have missed them if they'd been there the night before. He made a big show of yawning and stretching, sidling over to the window as he did so. Outside, on the sill, were two muddy scuff marks.

Later, while Ellie was in the bathroom, he fetched a tissue and cleaned them off. No sense in Mum worrying. He wasn't too worried himself. He'd made the same mistake before. Tell Ellie she couldn't do something and she'd go straight out and do it.

So Ellie had gone wandering in the dark, just to prove that girls have a bit of the werewolf in them, too. Big deal. She'd probably gone no further than the tool-shed at the bottom of the garden. But she had been out. He knew she had. She knew he knew she had. Perhaps now she'd made her point, she'd forget about it.

Two

Later that morning, Hal and Ellie and Dad walked down to the pub. All over the new estate, men in Marks and Spencer's sweaters were mowing already perfect lawns or giving their cars the kind of polish that made you wish you'd brought your sunglasses. It looked so much like any new estate in town, you couldn't help wondering why they'd gone to the trouble of moving to the country.

Then you turned the corner and there was old Laxworth village, battered survivor of a time when all mod cons meant no indoor bathroom or loo, just a brick privy at the end of the garden and a tin bath hanging on the wall. Here each house was defiantly different from its neighbours. Thatched roofs, tiled roofs and one of corrugated iron. Front doors painted respectable green or optimistic white or shocking pink.

Outside the Tiger's Head, the lawn was a battleground between grass and gravel which the gravel seemed to be winning. 'I don't know where it comes from,' the landlord would moan, as he shovelled it up and scattered more grass seed. A few days later, up the gravel would come again.

Here Mr Harding-Froggett liked to play the country gentleman on fine Sunday mornings. Whenever he wanted another drink, Mr Harding-Froggett would wave a twenty-pound note in the air, until the landlord spotted it through the window and came running to take his order.

Mr Harding-Froggett never went into the bar if he could help it. There were too many old men sitting there who still remembered him as plain Polly Froggett, whose poor old dad was found by the social worker lying ill in bed with a dead cow on the floor beside him. The ambulance had hardly turned the corner before young Polly was tearing down the old family homestead and putting up four Tudor bungalows in its place.

He was Mr Garth Harding-Froggett now, with a finger in more pies than Jack Horner. His half-timbered bungalows and Georgian maisonettes, plus five very profitable old people's homes, were scattered along the road from Laxworth to Melford. Oh, yes. Mr Garth Harding-Froggett was Somebody.

'What a wally!' remarked Ellie, plonking herself down on the low brick wall that edged the flowerbed outside the public bar. 'Why is he called Polly?' she asked Dad loudly, as he came out carrying their drinks and crisps.

'Sh!' said Dad.

'You were at school with him,' she persisted. 'You must know.'

Mr Garth Harding-Froggett gave no sign of having heard her, but he couldn't stop his ears from turning bright pink.

'Was he Pretty Polly? Or Polly Parrot?'

'Shut up, Ellie,' muttered Dad, 'or I'll swap those bacon crisps for cheese and onion *and* I'll make you eat them.' He lowered his voice still further. 'Pollywog is another word for tadpole. A tadpole is a young frog. So young Froggett's Polly Froggett. OK?'

'OK,' said Ellie sweetly.

Dad sauntered over to join the group round Polly Froggett, taking care to avoid Mr Froggett's dog, which was lurking under one of the iron tables. Mr Froggett had three dogs, all short-necked and bandy-legged like himself, and all so bad-tempered that if they couldn't find anyone else to fight, they used to fight each other. On Sunday mornings, he would sort out the least damaged one, drag it down to the pub and tie it to a table leg.

As the landlord appeared in the doorway carrying a tray of drinks, Hal's fingers found a pebble in the flowerbed behind him. He weighed it carefully in his hand, then tossed it so that it landed on the far side of the dog.

The dog ambled over to check it out. By the time it had decided it wasn't something to eat, the landlord was safely past. The dog gave Hal a sour look and crawled back under the table.

Hal grinned to himself and glanced at Ellie. But though Ellie was watching the dog with her eyes, she wasn't really seeing it. She was too busy listening. Listening to the conversation through the open window of the bar behind them, with a knowing expression on her face. As Hal tuned in his ears to listen too, he felt the hackles rising on his neck.

'It was just a dog you seen,' someone was saying. 'Just an ol' dog, looking a bit strange in the moonlight.'

'I know what a dog look like, boy. I weren't so far

gone I wouldn't a' known a dog if I seen one. Sheep know what a dog look like. Know what he smell like, too. If that a' been a dog, you'd a' heard they sheep hollerin' from here to Melford.'

'What you reckon it was, then?'

'I don't know. I'm just telling you what I seen. I ain't goin' up there again.'

'Too late, boy,' another voice broke in, quiet and sinister. 'If you seen what I think you seen, you ain't long for this world.' There was a puzzled silence, broken by the same voice. 'A creature like a dog, you say?'

'Bit like a dog. Nearer the ground, like.'

'Staring eyes? Fiery-looking?'

'I never seen its eyes. Never said I did.'

'Never mind. Makes no difference. You know what I reckon? I reckon it was Black Shuck you saw. Didn't your old grannie never warn you about Black Shuck? You seen even the tail of Black Shuck, it means you ain't long for this world.'

'Don't think it had much of a tail,' said the original speaker doubtfully. Then it slowly dawned on him that it was all a wind-up. 'I was only telling you what I saw,' he protested over the laughter. 'Something that didn't ought to be there.'

And all the time Ellie sat there with a smug I-know-something-they-don't-know look on her face.

'Ellie . . .' Hal began.

But at that moment, Mia, eldest daughter of the Stittle tribe, hove into view from one of the narrow alleyways that passed for side-streets in that part of the village. She was wearing a short, black knitted skirt, so tight it looked as if it had started life as a sleeve, and a plastic bomber jacket so big, you could have put a whole bomber crew inside and still got the zip done up. Her stiletto heels tit-tupped along the pavement like the sound of Blind Pew coming to deliver the black spot. The men outside the Tiger's Head froze with their pint mugs halfway to their lips. The dog crawled further under the table.

Mia swept past, ignoring them all, her heels stabbing angry little holes in the grass and gravel. The bar fell silent as she flung open the door. Seconds later, she was out again, dragging her husband Lemmy behind her, until she had room to swing her handbag.

Luckily, Lemmy was a lot taller than she was. It caught him just below the shoulder, knocking him off balance. Mia followed up with a left jab which caught him full on the nose, before he had the presence of mind to sink to the ground and stay there. The Stittles never hit a man when he was down. It was more fun to let him get up, then knock him down again.

'Where you bin?' she demanded. 'I've had 'em all out looking for you since before breakfast. Didn't I tell you you was to always come straight home? Didn't I tell him?' she appealed to the world at large.

Some of the men nodded. The rest went on staring into their beer, like gypsies at a crystal-ball gazing competition.

Without a glance at Mia, Ellie got up, walked over to Lemmy and handed him the lace handkerchief Aunt May had brought back from Malta. (The one supposed to be for show, not blow.) Lemmy took it gratefully and mopped his bleeding nose.

Mia sucked in her breath until Hal thought she might burst. Her fat little feet pawed the ground. Then she suddenly let the breath out again, with a sound like letting go of a balloon, turned and stalked off down the street.

Lemmy got up and shambled after her, taking with him Ellie's little bit of lace. The dog stuck its head out from under the table and tried a menacing growl. Lemmy, eyes fixed on Mia's back, might as well have been deaf. The dog retreated, disappointed.

People were moving about again, restarting conversations, when Ellie blew up her empty crisp packet and burst it. The dog leapt so high, it almost knocked itself silly on the table. Then it rushed round and round, barking, until its lead got wrapped round the table legs and pulled it up short.

People everywhere were mopping up the drinks they'd spilt over their best Sunday casuals and making rude remarks about kids in pubs. Most of them seemed to be looking at Hal, which he thought was very unfair. But Mr Harding-Froggett turned and grinned at Ellie. And he winked!

'You've got an admirer,' grinned Hal.

'Huh!' said Ellie. 'He's a waste of space!'

'Home!' said Dad.

That afternoon, Frank Finnegan (ace reporter of the *Melford Mercury*) dropped in to see Dad. As usual, he managed to time things so that he arrived just as they were having tea. Mum had fastened Jack into his high chair and put a chocolate finger biscuit on the tray to tempt him, when the doorbell rang. She answered it. When she saw who it was, she said nothing, but went to fetch another cup, leaving Frank to find his own way.

'God bless all here!' he announced himself cheerfully. 'Still on the banana diet, Jack?' He picked up the chocolate biscuit. 'You don't want this, then?' Jack shook his head. 'Ah, well, waste not, want not.' He popped the biscuit into his own mouth. 'My favourite,' he said.

Mum came back with the extra cup. She glanced from Jack to Frank and back again. Tutted to herself and put another biscuit in front of the baby. Jack grabbed it and held it tight. He wasn't going to eat it, but neither was anyone else.

Frank took the cup that Mum held out to him. 'I'm a terrible nuisance, I know, Ba,' he said. He kissed her lightly on the mouth before straddling a chair cowboy-fashion and turning to Dad. 'Well, Dan, did you see our man?'

Dad nodded.

'And?'

'He's willing enough. But he doesn't want to be the first.'

Mum looked from one to the other. 'You two are up to something.' Yes, thought Hal, Frank's up to something. Some story he's got his teeth into . . .

33

'Who are you *talking* about?' demanded Mum, but she was smiling. She could never be annoyed with Frank for long. Ellie seemed to be trying to thread herself through the rungs of his chair. Yes, everybody liked Frank. So why don't I? Hal wondered.

'I know!' announced Ellie. 'I know! It's Polly-Wally-Froggett, isn't it?'

'It is,' said Frank. 'We're doing this series for the *Mercury* on local houses and the people who live there. We thought we'd kick off with Polly Froggett's place.'

'You ought to do Gran's house,' said Ellie. 'That's heaps more interesting. Gran can tell you all about it.'

'It used to be a weaver's cottage,' put in Hal.

'It used to be a pub,' said Ellie.

'You can see the marks of the pegs on the wall, where they used to measure out the wool for weaving.'

'They used to get all their water from the pond in the garden. Tadpoles and waterweed and all!'

'Dad was born on the kitchen table, weren't you, Dad?'

'I can't say I remember,' said Dad.

'And Polly-Wally-Froggett was desperate to buy it and get Gran to move into one of his old people's homes, but she told him to get stuffed.'

'Ellie!' said Mum. 'I'm sure she didn't.'

'Bet she did,' said Ellie.

I bet she did, too, thought Hal.

Frank Finnegan listened with a smile on his face and you could tell he hadn't been listening at all, because he suddenly said, 'How about the old Manor House, Dan?'

'Miss Letty's?' A wide grin spread over Dad's face. 'I don't think you've met Miss Letty Harding?'

Everybody in Laxworth knew Miss Letty Harding. Tall and gaunt, dressed in floppy trousers and jackets to match, she looked like a forties' film star, but with a voice trained on the hunting field. Hal had stood behind her in the village shop while she gave her weekly order to Mr Singh. The supermarket in Melford was cheaper, but Miss Letty never used it. 'If we don't patronise our village shop,' she said, 'we'll lose it. And then what will happen to the poor old things who don't have cars to run them into town whenever they want a loaf of bread? Besides, the village shop delivers.'

It would never have occurred to Mr Singh to tell

her that he'd long ago given up delivering to anyone else.

'Miss Letitia Harding,' said Dad, 'is a lady. She's not going to let the likes of us spread snippets of her family history and pictures of her dearest possessions all over the local rag.'

'Leave it to me, Dan. I'll use a bit of the old Irish charm.'

'Don't lay it on too thick,' advised Dad. 'Miss Letty may have lived all her life in Laxworth, but I daresay she can tell a London accent from an Irish brogue.'

'It's not in the brogue, Dan. It's in the blood! I'll sweet-talk the old lady. No problem.'

Nobody had taken any notice of Jack for quite some time. The biscuit had vanished and there was chocolate round his mouth. Hal slid another biscuit on to the tray and looked away. Jack picked it up and absent-mindedly began to chew it.

The sky was clouding over when Frank Finnegan left. Soon big drops of rain began to fall. By bedtime it was pouring down in quantities that would have had Noah phoning his gopher-wood supplier.

Hal was relieved. Even Ellie wasn't daft enough to go wandering about in that. For a long time he stood at the window, watching the rain pouring down out of a darkening sky. Beyond the twilight lay a different world. A world where things changed their shape and creatures lurked that never saw the light of day. Where imagined fears took shape from the shadows and lived a life of their own.

He went to bed but he couldn't sleep for the thoughts that kept tumbling around in his head. Monkey thoughts, Gran would have called them. Thoughts of Ellie and fear of the night. What was it the man in the pub had seen? Ellie knew. Ellie wasn't afraid. 'Nothing to be afraid of,' Gran had told them. 'Are you afraid of Uncle Ho?'

Uncle Ho, wandering by owl-light among the wild, lonely places, becoming more himself. And something else, still forming itself out of the mist and shadows, lurking among the sheep. The sheep weren't frightened. The sheep weren't frightened, but the man was. 'He made up stories to frighten himself,' Gran had said, 'about a creature that was half-man, half-wolf.'

Polly Froggett and his dogs, looking so alike. Had he chosen the dogs because they looked like him? Or had he and the dogs both changed so that they became more like one another? Things don't change their shape. But pollywogs turn into frogs. Tails vanish, legs grow, gills are replaced by lungs . . .

Caterpillars turn into butterflies. And no one knows how or when they do it. Open up a chrysalis – no, don't! Because you'll never find an ex-caterpillar or an almost-butterfly. All you'll find is a horrible, soggy mess. Yet, in the dark, it changes . . .

Monkey thoughts.

My sister is not a werewolf. It sounded daft. As daft as 'my sister has not got two heads'. Of course she hadn't. So what was she doing out there in the dark? What was out there?

Monkey thoughts, chasing each other round and round; playing leapfrog; standing themselves on their heads; putting two and two together and making twenty-two. He was glad when it was morning.

Three

Through the window of the school bus, Hal saw the Stittles walking up the hill, with the dogged look of the Clantons heading for the OK Corral.

First the twins, Harrison and Dustin, kicking an empty Coke can between them. Then Rutger, giving a piggy-back to Madonna. After him tottered Michelle, in a pair of platform shoes that must have been passed down from Mia. It was nearly four miles from their house to school. If she'd been anyone but a Stittle, Hal would have said she wasn't going to make it. Last came Dolph, thinking his own dark thoughts. He was the one who'd got them thrown off the bus again the week before, for setting fire to the back seat.

The Stittles had protested his innocence. If Dolph had meant to start a fire, they said, the bus would be a burnt-out wreck by now. The smell of burning came from the herbal mixture old Mr Stittle had given him for his asthma. The driver pointed to the *No Smoking* sign and threw them off anyway.

So for a while the Stittles walked to school and back. All of them. It was the only time none of them bunked off. They stuck together, the Stittles. Their view of life was simple. It was the Stittles v. the Rest of the World. In a way, Hal envied them.

All through morning school, those monkey thoughts kept coming back to tease him.

'You're away with the fairies,' said Miss Campbell, during maths, when she found him doing the questions on page twenty-three instead of the ones on page thirty-two. He'd got them all wrong, too. Three weeks ago, he'd got most of them right.

Mr Boot, the head teacher, took them for history.

'A historian,' he said, 'has to be a kind of detective. Today, we're going to be historical detectives. We're going to reopen a murder case. The case of the Princes in the Tower. Two little boys, younger than you, locked up in the Tower of London and murdered –' his gaze lingered thoughtfully on the Stittle twins, Harrison and Dustin – 'horribly murdered, on the orders of their wicked uncle, King Richard the Third. So we are told. But was Richard guilty? How can.we know?'

'I bet he was framed,' said Harrison Stittle firmly.

'Fitted up,' agreed Dustin.

'If that turns out to be the case,' said Mr Boot, 'then we have to ask, who by?'

'The police, o'course,' said Dustin, quick as a flash.

'Stands to reason,' said Harrison.

'Did he make a statement?' asked Dustin.

Mr Boot sighed. 'No, Dustin, he did not make a statement.'

'Never make a statement,' Harrison advised the class.

'Don't make it easy for 'em,' said Dustin.

'You gotta right to silence.'

'No, you haven't,' Dustin contradicted him. 'Not any more.'

'They can't make you say anything, not if you don't want.'

'S'pose not,' Dustin agreed. 'Say nuthin'.'

'They got no evidence, they gotta let you go.'

'Evidence!' Mr Boot grabbed for the word as it sailed by, like a drowning man catching at a passing lump of wood. 'Let's look at the evidence. The facts. Five hundred years ago . . .'

Evidence, thought Hal. Facts. That was what he needed, to put those monkey thoughts in their place.

He was on first sitting for dinner that week, but he decided to put off the big decision – sausage and mash or vegetable moussaka? – and go to the library first, while it was quiet. He found Mrs Utterley, the librarian, sitting alone with a solitary apple on the desk in front of her.

'I will get thinner,' she murmured, eyes half-closed. 'I *will* get thinner. I *will* get thinner!'

Hal couldn't imagine Mrs Utterley getting thinner, any more than his old teddy bear. He stood patiently waiting for her to notice him. When she did, she gave a start and blushed as red as the apple. 'Oh! Hello. Need some help?'

'I want to find out something about – wolves?' Wolves was where it had all begun – or werewolves. He had an idea that Mrs Utterley would look less kindly on a request for information about werewolves.

'Wolves,' repeated Mrs Utterley. 'Is it for a project?'

Mrs Utterley loved projects. If a class was doing a project, she would drive off to the county library and come back with boxfuls of stuff to help. She spent hours cutting articles out of newspapers and magazines and filing them in big metal cabinets, in case they came in handy one day for a project.

'It's not for a project,' Hal confessed. 'I'm just interested.'

Mrs Utterley gave a hungry glance at the apple. But duty called. 'Let's start with the encyclopaedia,' she suggested. 'After that, you do know how to use the catalogue, don't you? Was there anything special you wanted to know?'

'No. Just wolves in general.' He tried to make his voice sound casual. 'Things like – are there any wolves in England nowadays?'

'Wild ones, you mean? 'Fraid not. I think the last one was killed in the reign of Henry the Fifth. Or was it Henry the Eighth? There used to be a reward for killing a wolf, you see – as much as for killing an outlaw. "Wolf's head" used to be another word for outlaw. Did you know that? Ah! Here we are: the last wolf in England was killed in about fifteen hundred. That would be Henry the Seventh. I knew it was one of the Henrys.'

'How did they know?'

'How did they know what?'

'How did they know it was the last one?'

'I see what you mean. They didn't have David Attenborough beavering about, telling everyone this was an endangered species, did they?'

'What about Black Shuck?'

'Ah, now, Black Shuck's a different kettle of fish altogether. He's more of a legend. Sort of a harbinger of doom. What sparked off this interest, anyway?'

Hal shrugged. 'I was just interested. I'll have a look in the catalogue, shall I?'

He found a book on wolves. It was very thin and mostly pictures, but he checked it out. Then he took advantage of a bunch of first years arriving in search of Enid Blytons and Roald Dahls to slip round to the end of the fiction section, where the books of folk tales were kept.

Gran had said that people used to make up stories about werewolves. So what were the stories? Where were they? He leafed through the books, one at a time. He found stories of people turned into frogs, pigs or swans; horses and dragons; cats, dogs, bears and even butterflies. He found people who were half-horses, half-fish, half-lions. (Were-horses, were-fish and were-lions, if you like). But not a single wolf.

There was Red Riding Hood's wolf, of course. But that was just a wolf. A talking wolf. A talking animal was nothing special, not in that sort of story.

So what about werewolves, then?

He might have missed it, if the book hadn't been so old, it was falling apart. A picture fell out on to the floor. He bent to pick it up and saw that it showed a creature half-man half-wolf. A wolf on its way to becoming a man, head and shoulders lifting out of the wolf's skin, like a swimmer rising out of the sea.

The story wasn't called *The Werewolf*. It was called *Bisclavret*. Inside the book's front cover someone had written:

If this book should chance to roam,
Box its ears and send it home
To
Miss Letitia Rose Harding,
The Manor House,
Laxworth,
Suffolk,
England,
Great Britain,
Europe,
The World.

The first years were jostling round Mrs Utterley's

desk, in a hurry to have their books checked out, so as not to be late for their dinners.

Hal slipped the werewolf book underneath the other one and walked out. Boys don't read folk tales. Besides, there was a queue. He wasn't stealing it. He'd bring it back as soon as he'd finished with it and just put it back on the shelf, no questions asked.

Alone again at last, Mrs Utterley looked for her apple, but it wasn't there. One of the first years had taken it.

That evening, lying on his bed, Hal took out the book and read the story of Bisclavret.

Now I will tell you a tale of the one the Breton folk call Le Bisclavret, which in English is the werewolf.

A man cannot choose to be a werewolf and he cannot choose not to be. On nights when the moon shines bright, if the wolf blood is in him, he will feel his palms begin to itch and he will lift up his head and howl and howl until someone lets him out.

There was a nobleman who was just such a one. He never told his wife how it was with him, but each time stole away, leaving his clothes in a safe place, so that he could return to his man-shape when morning came.

Time and again she asked him where he went on those nights when he was not with her. At last, one night, she followed him and in the moonlight saw her husband slip off his clothes – saw his body all covered with hair – saw him lift up his head and bay at the moon – saw him drop on all fours and bound away into the shadows.

Poor lady! What could she do? Whom could she tell?

She told the man her husband thought was his dearest friend. 'What shall I do?' she sobbed.

'Rid yourself of him without delay,' the false friend said. 'There is no need to kill him. Next time he is in his wolf's shape, take away his clothes and burn them. Without them, he cannot become a man again.'

She did as he told her, except that she did not burn the clothes, but hid them away. She let it be known that her husband had gone out hunting alone and not returned. He must have had an accident – been wounded – dead.

After a decent time, she married the false friend.

The werewolf lived a wretched life in the forest. He tried to live as much like a man as he could, taking for his food nuts and berries and wild birds' eggs, but he was often hungry. Sometimes it rained and sometimes it snowed and he was hard put to it to find a dry hole into which to crawl.

One day the king came to the forest to hunt.

The werewolf was so muddled now between his man-nature and his wolf-nature that he thought he might go to the king and ask for justice. He forgot that a wolf cannot speak. When he came to the king, he could only lie down, whimpering softly. The king said he would keep this gentle wolf as a pet.

The wolf was almost ready to forget that he had ever been a man by the time the hunting party arrived at his old home. There stood his wife and his false friend, waiting to welcome the king to the home that had once been his.

Suddenly all his man's anger welled up inside him. Without so much as a growl of warning, he leapt at the false friend and tore out his throat, killing him where he stood. Then the wolf was quiet again.

There is something strange here, thought the king.

Long after the rest of the castle was asleep, the lady lay awake, listening to the wolf prowling the corridors, searching, searching, until she could bear it no longer. She took her husband's clothes from the old chest where she had hidden them and crept downstairs to burn them.

Too late! The wolf set up such a howling that men came running from all over the castle. There stood the wolf, with his back to the fire. There stood the lady, with her husband's clothes in her hand.

The king looked from one to the other. 'Put down the clothes,' he said. Then he ordered that the wolf be left alone till morning.

In the first light of day they found the nobleman, dressed in his clothes, almost as they remembered him, but older, thinner, sadder.

The king asked him, 'What shall we do with this wife of yours? By law, she should be burned alive.'

'By man's law, yes,' said the nobleman. 'But a wolf kills only for food. With a man's anger I killed the man who was once my friend. I am sorry for it now. The woman cannot harm me. Let her go.'

So the lady was sent away to a nunnery to repent her sins. The man lived on quietly and sadly, almost alone.

But on nights when the moon shone bright, he would feel his palms begin to itch, he would lift up his head and bay at the moon and go running free through the woods and over the hills until daybreak. Then he was happy again.

And that is the tale of Bisclavret, the werewolf.

Poor old Bisclavret! thought Hal. He wasn't scary, just sad. It was the werewolf's man-nature, not his wolf-nature that made him kill the false friend. Was that right? That wolves only kill when they're hungry? He picked up the other book and began flicking through it.

Wolves turned out to be quite interesting.

A lone wolf is a rare creature. Most wolves live in families, all helping to look after the little ones. Taking it in turns to baby-sit, while the others go off and hunt. Bringing back food, ready chewed, to make it easy for the cubs to swallow. Wolves need other wolves to help them hunt, working like sheep-dogs, cutting out their quarry from the herd and running it down.

And when the wolves have eaten their fill, they howl, inviting the smaller animals to feast on what's left over, foxes and mice, birds, squirrels, butterflies and beetles. Native Americans say that when the wolf eats, no one goes hungry. They admire the wolf for his generosity and courage.

There is no record of a healthy wolf ever killing a human being. But from time immemorial, men have hunted wolves.

Poor lonely creatures they must have been, the last few wolves in England. Lonely and hungry and bewildered, as men hunted them to extinction, for fun, for money, or for their pelts. From picture after picture, the wolves stared at him, thin grey faces, eyes sad and knowing, almost as if they remembered.

Hal leaned back and closed his eyes and tried to imagine himself as Bisclavret, lord of the animals. Lord of the night. Running through the wild, lonely places, alone and unafraid. If only! In his heart, he knew he'd always be afraid of the dark.

But that night he slept well. And the next.

On Wednesday evening Frank Finnegan came round to see Dad. Mum was upstairs, putting Jack to bed. Ellie was out somewhere. Hal was sitting curled up with a book when he heard Frank's voice. 'You were right about Miss Letty, Dan. There's no sweet-talking her.'

Dad's voice, almost relieved: 'It's no go then?'

Frank gave a chuckle. 'On the contrary! She'll help us in any way she can.' He shouldered his way into the living-room and helped himself to an apple. 'Such a pair of eyes she has, Dan! Such a head on her shoulders! Why did no man ever snap her up?'

'I rather think she frightened them all off.'

' "Are you a gambling man?" she says. How am I

supposed to know whether she's strictly anti or running a poker school and looking for one more to make up the numbers? I had to take a gamble on the answer. "No, ma'am," says I. "I am not a gambler." She looked at me with those blue eyes of hers and I could see what she was thinking: a gambler and a liar, too. "Well, come in anyway," she said. And I knew there was nothing for it but to be straight with her. It's all arranged. She'll let us do the piece on the old Manor House, then set up the meeting at Polly Froggett's. While you're taking your pictures I can have a good look round ... They're there, Dan! They've got to be!'

Dad glanced at Hal.

'Let's talk about it over a drink,' he said. 'I'll tell Ba.'

Hal heard him going upstairs. Mum stopped singing to Jack and there was a murmur of voices.

Frank Finnegan perched himself on the arm of the chair opposite Hal. 'Good book?'

' 'Sall right,' said Hal.

Frank sat, tapping his foot, drumming his fingers on his knee. 'Once upon a time,' he said. 'I was going to be the great investigative journalist. Exposing crime and corruption wherever I found it! You know?'

Hal nodded.

'Either that, or Our Man in Beirut. Or Afghanistan. Wherever there was trouble. Danger. But even in a little place like this, you can find a story, if you take the trouble to look . . .'

Then Dad came downstairs and he and Frank went out together.

On Friday night Ellie went wandering in the moonlight again. Hal was suddenly wide awake. He went to the window and drew back the curtains and looked down into the garden. Ellie was walking across the lawn, away from the house. He opened the window and called softly, 'Ellie!' She gave no sign of having heard him. She walked on, making for the shed.

Quickly he pulled on jeans and a sweatshirt. No socks. Flip-flops on his feet. Quicker than trainers. No laces. Less easy to climb in, though. He lost one, getting down on to the roof of the utility room and had to scrabble for it in the shadows. When he looked up again, Ellie had gone.

He was alone. Alone in the dark. No, not alone! Ellie couldn't be far away. 'Ellie! Please!' (But softly, so as not to wake Mum and Dad). 'Ellie!'

No answer.

'Ellie, you pig! I'll get you for this!'

That's right: get angry. He closed his eyes. I am Bisclavret, he told himself, alone in the dark and unafraid. I am Bisclavret, the wolf. Get angry. Go after her.

What was he afraid of? The moonlight was almost as bright as day. He could make out every bush, every flower in the garden, right to the rockery at the far end. So why did they all look so unreal?

Just climb down on to the coal bunker, then to the ground. Cross the lawn and he'd find her waiting in the shed.

The air struck cold. The grass was wet, brushing against his feet like tiny tongues. The night was full of the whisperings of an unseen world going about its business, falling silent as he passed, listening and watching for every move he made.

He reached the shed and flung open the door. Ellie wasn't there. Only her trainers, just inside, placed neatly side by side. Hal picked them up and looked at them, puzzled. Why on earth would she take off her trainers?

He thought of Bisclavret, the werewolf, taking off his clothes and his wife hiding them, so he couldn't turn back into a man. Perhaps Ellie thought you could make the change bit by bit, feet first. Once you got the feet right, the rest would follow. If he took her trainers away, would she turn up for breakfast with little, furry wolf-feet? What would Mum say? He chuckled at the thought.

Then he heard it. The creature! Just the other side of the chain-link fence, snuffling and scratching at the ground. All this time it had been there, watching him, listening.

He couldn't see it properly, because of the shadow thrown by the shed. But it was big. Big and dark – almost black. A flash of white. Then the creature was running, running across the common, crouching low.

Hal dropped the shoes and he was running, too. Running in the opposite direction, back to his warm, safe bed, with the covers drawn up over his head. Not that that would be much protection against the Thing that was out there!

It was easy in the cold light of day to say you didn't believe such stuff. But the night was a different world, where the same rules didn't apply. He believed now. Yes, he believed! Believed in werewolves and Black Shuck and the Tooth Fairy and little green men from Mars! He believed! He believed.

And then he slept.

Next morning he went down to the end of the garden and looked over the fence at the place where the creature had been. The earth was scuffed, as though something had been trying to dig its way in. Further away, as it made off across the common, it had left two clear pawprints before it reached the rough grass. Each of them showed five toes, or fingers, very like a human hand. But the marks of the claws were almost half as long again.

Ellie was watching him, with that knowing look she'd worn before, when they overheard the men talking in the pub.

'Ellie,' said Hal. 'You've got to promise me —'

'Promise you what?' she asked, all innocence.

'It's not safe out here in the dark. You've got to promise —'

Ellie started to giggle. Then she turned and ran back towards the house.

'Or I'll have to tell Mum!' Hal shouted after her.

It was his bad luck that Mum appeared in the kitchen doorway just at that moment, carrying a basket of washing to hang out. 'Tell me what?' she asked.

'Nothing,' mumbled Hal, head down, pushing past her.

In the book on wolves he'd borrowed from the library there was a life-size picture of a wolf's pawprint. It was nothing like the marks at the bottom of the garden. Four pads, not five. Short-clawed.

Ellie stuck her head round the bedroom door. 'If you tell Mum,' she hissed, 'I'm not speaking to you ever again!' Then she was gone.

Later that morning, Hal walked down again to the bottom of the garden. Someone had smoothed out the paw marks and stamped the ground down hard. There was nothing to show that they'd ever been there. Hal sighed. What he needed to do was talk to Gran. Luckily today was Saturday.

Four

Hal had forgotten it was the first Saturday in the month. Three and sometimes four Saturdays in a row he and Ellie cycled round to Gran's on their own. But on the first Saturday of each month, Mum strapped Jack into his push-chair and they all went, taking the short cut across the common. The way meandered more like a stream than a public footpath, skirting every tree and bush and clump of nettles. To Jack, at push-chair level, it must be like a safari through uncharted jungle.

Everywhere, like the traces of some savage tribe, lay evidence of the Stittles: tunnels leading away into the undergrowth; a small cairn of stones; a shallow hollow in the ground, with the ashes of a fire; a tree hung with dead birds, voles, strings of old milk-bottle tops that glittered and rustled in the wind, several ancient strips of cloth and one football sock.

Just short of the road, where it should have carried straight on to come out directly opposite Gran's house, the path turned sharp right through the edge of the wood, finally emerging into the lane a hundred metres further up.

There, in the woods, they lost Ellie.

'Ellie!' Mum called, and called again. 'Ellie!' She looked about and fussed and said, 'I hope she doesn't wander into the road.' As if Ellie was no more than four years old.

Nearly ten minutes later, Ellie suddenly appeared. 'Sorry. Were you calling me? I was just picking some flowers for Gran.' Among the mass of cow parsley, which made it look a lot, Hal counted three celandines and two very tired bluebells. He also noticed the dirt under her fingernails.

'That's nice,' said Mum. 'But don't wander off again. Stay where I can see you.'

All down the lane, Ellie kept an eye open for any patch of colour, diving into the roadside grasses to pick dead-nettles, clover or meadowsweet, so that she ended up with quite a sizeable bunch to present to Gran.

'We'd better put these in water right away,' said Gran.

As far as Hal could see, the flowers had lost the will to live by now, but Gran filled a vase with water and solemnly took them a few at a time. 'What have we got here? Celandines. And what's this?'

'Stitchwort,' said Ellie.

'That's right. Here's a violet! It's late for violets. Where did you find it? Smell that meadowsweet! I shall save that and dry it for my pot pourri.'

This gave Mum plenty of time to examine the room for hidden mantraps before she let Jack out of his push-chair. Try as she might, she couldn't find fault. The guard was in place in front of the Aga; every breakable object well out of reach; the floor was scrubbed so clean not even Mum could object to Jack walking, sitting, crawling or even eating his tea on it.

Gran did her best on these monthly visits, to live up to Mum's idea of what a gran should be. She put on a skirt and a clean, white blouse and sat with her knees together. The table was laid for tea with china cups (and saucers), home-made cake and scones and strawberry jam. The cucumber sandwiches, in neat triangles, with the crusts cut off, were a bit OTT, thought Hal. Sometimes it seemed as if the whole of Gran's Little Old Lady act was a bit over the top. As if she was playing a game for Mum's benefit. Every now and then, she couldn't help teasing. When Mum said something about no need to go to so much trouble, Gran said meekly that she never went to any more trouble than she felt like going to. Then she added brightly, 'Who was it who said that the dust doesn't get any worse after the first four years?'

Mum's worried gaze shifted from the floor to the mantelpiece, where nothing seemed to have been moved in all the Saturdays they'd been coming. Cyril the squirrel (shot and stuffed by Gran's father) still rubbed shoulders with the Dresden shepherdess. The sheep's skull Ellie had found on the common still leaned up against the antique marble clock with the gilded cherubs which had stopped long, long ago at five past seven. Propped up at one end was a photo of Gran, carrying a *Ban the Bomb* banner, flanked by a clergyman in a beret and an old man with a face like a horse, who had both been quite famous in their day.

What always fascinated Hal about the picture was Dad, in his push-chair, looking dead embarrassed.

Imagine being embarrassed by your mother when you're only two!

At the other end of the mantelpiece was a framed picture cut from a newspaper of Gran being arrested outside the American Embassy in Grosvenor Square. She said it took six policemen to carry her.

'And of course, I have Lemmy to help me in the garden,' Gran was saying.

Mum looked uneasily through the open doorway towards the vegetable patch, where Lemmy was earthing up the potatoes. 'Stittles!' she muttered, as if all that was wrong with the world would suddenly be put right if only there were no Stittles in it.

Hal decided it wasn't worth pointing out that Lemmy wasn't really a Stittle. You could tell that just by looking at him. Stittles were fair and squat. Lemmy was tall and dark and gangling.

Nobody quite knew who Lemmy was. Perhaps he was a runaway from a children's home. Perhaps he'd been left behind by a travelling fair. One day he'd turned up in the village and attached himself to the Stittles. And instead of thumping him, the Stittles took him home and trained him up and married him off to Mia as soon as they were both old enough.

Now he was known as Lemmy Stittle. Married to the Mob.

'Where's Jack?' Mum asked suddenly.

'I'll find him,' offered Hal, glad of an excuse to escape. Ellie had wandered off already, without bothering about excuses.

Jack didn't take much finding. He was sitting at the end of the lawn, with his fat little legs stretched out in front of him. Near by, Lemmy worked on, shovelling the earth with easy, relaxed movements.

'What have you got there, Jack?' asked Hal, seeing Jack clutching something in his hand.

Lemmy paused briefly in his digging and looked at Hal with his slow, shy smile. 'Tha's just a few peas,' he said. 'Peas come on early over by the wall, there. Sun brings 'em on.' He went back to his work.

'Aren't you lucky, Jack?' said Hal. 'First peas of the season. Can I have one?'

Jack opened his hand, selected a pea and gave it to Hal. Then he stuffed the rest in his mouth in case Hal had any ideas about asking for another one.

'Thanks, Jack,' said Hal. The pea tasted mainly of Jack's hot little hand, but Hal swallowed it manfully.

Jack was already crawling away in search of pastures new. He could walk, of course, but life

63

tended to be more interesting the nearer you were to the ground. You got to see things other people didn't see. Like caterpillars. A big, green caterpillar!

Jack reached out to grab it, but Lemmy was quicker. He looked Jack in the eye, raised a finger to his lips, then opened up his hand to show the caterpillar, which set off across his palm in search of food.

Gently, Lemmy picked it up and placed it on Jack's hand. Jack giggled as it tickled him, but he held it steady with his hand out flat, just as Lemmy had done.

Hal picked a few clover leaves and laid them on Jack's hand. 'Caterpillar,' he said. 'That's a caterpillar, Jack.' The caterpillar started to explore among the leaves.

Then Mum swooped down like Superman, out of nowhere, to whisk Jack out of danger. 'What are you doing?' she demanded, as she picked him up.

Hal and Lemmy said nothing. The question wasn't for them. It was for Jack, but Jack's English wasn't up to it.

'Puller,' he said, proud to have learned a new word, holding out his hand to show her. He grinned, showing a trace of something green at the corner of his mouth.

'You haven't been letting him eat grass?' exclaimed Mum. 'Oh! There's a caterpillar! Drop it, Jack. Spit it out.'

Jack yelled and squirmed in Mum's arms, almost turning upside down in his efforts to see where his 'puller' had fallen.

'It's all right, Mum,' said Hal. 'It was just a few peas. Lemmy gave him a few peas to eat, that's all. Don't move, Mum, or you'll step on it.' He retrieved the caterpillar and showed it to Jack. 'He's got to go home now. OK, Jack? Say bye-bye, caterpillar.'

Jack said nothing, but he stopped yelling as Mum stalked back to the house with him. Lemmy gave Hal a sympathetic smile and went back to his work.

Hal was putting the caterpillar back among the long grass when he saw Ellie coming out of the tool-shed, carrying a trowel and a sack. Where was she off to?

He followed her out of the garden and across the road, diving into the undergrowth at the far side, where he was astonished to find a sort of path. A path for dwarfs, maybe – there were branches growing across it no more than a metre above the ground – but a path, nevertheless, and regularly used.

Burrs stuck to his clothes and brambles snagged them, but Hal crept on, bending double, treading silently on the dead leaves. He listened for Ellie rustling through the undergrowth ahead of him, but there wasn't a sound. Not a bird singing, not a mouse stirring, as if the whole wood was holding its breath. He could hear his heart pounding, his breath hissing, only it didn't sound like him – more like someone close beside him. His eyes played tricks, creating faces out of sunlight and shadow, watching and waiting . . .

Of course, there wasn't really anything to be afraid of. He was just winding himself up. All the same, it was pretty spooky. *I am Bisclavret, lord of the forest* . . .

Something was waiting on the path ahead of him, sitting patiently. Hal froze. And then he recognised . . . Uncle Ho!

'Stupid cat!'

Uncle Ho growled softly, swishing his tail, then vanished into the shadows again.

Hal came out into a clearing beside a bank of earth, with alder trees above it, where Ellie was digging. Digging like mad with the trowel. Shovelling loose earth into the sack.

'Don't just stand there,' she said. 'Come and help me. You hold the bag. I'll dig.'

Hal did as he was told for a bit, then, 'Do you mind telling me why we're doing this?' he asked.

'We're hiding the evidence,' panted Ellie. Her face was pink and shiny and her hair was coming loose, but she still kept on digging like fury.

'Evidence of what?' asked Hal.

'Digging.'

'So why did you dig here in the first place?'

'It wasn't me, you great girl's blouse! It's them!' She pointed with the trowel towards a hole in the bank beside them. Further on, Hal noticed two more. Too big for rabbits.

'Foxes?' he guessed.

'Does it smell like foxes?' demanded Ellie.

He shrugged.

'It's badgers,' said Ellie. 'Gran said I'd got to tell you. So now I've told you, right?'

'Badgers? How do you know?'

'Because I've seen them.' Ellie took a rest from digging and sat down, drawing her knees up, with her arms wrapped round them. 'Friday and Saturday nights. Gran won't let me come the rest of the week, because of school next day.'

'Badgers! You were watching badgers. That's where you were off to! That's what it was among the sheep! That's what I saw!'

'What did you think it was?' Ellie giggled. 'A wolf?'

'No, I —' Of course, she'd seen the books in his room.

'You did! You did!' Ellie hugged her knees in delight. 'No wonder you ran! You gave poor Aunt May such a fright!'

'Aunt May?' What had Aunt May got to do with it? Last time they'd heard from Aunt May, she was off on her travels again, sailing up the Nile on an Arab felucca. 'What if it hadn't been me that saw you?' he demanded. 'What if Mum or Dad had woken up?'

'Mum never wakes. Dad knows. Gran wouldn't let me come until I told him. He said it's all right, as long as I'm with Gran. She used to take him badger-watching in the olden days. There were lots more of them then. Then horrible Polly Froggett bought the land and sent men round to gas them.'

'Why?'

'He said they were giving his cows some horrible disease. But where did the badgers catch it from, if it wasn't from his silly cows? He murdered them and they hadn't done anything!' She brushed away angry tears. 'There haven't been badgers here for years and years. So now we've got to keep it a secret.'

Ellie lay down with her ear close against the bank. She smiled and beckoned Hal over. 'Listen,' she said.

Hal put his ear to the ground. A snuffling and an indistinct muttering came from under the earth, like Dad when he fell asleep in front of the telly.

'That's Father William,' said Ellie. 'Sometimes you can hear the cubs playing up and down the tunnels.'

Hal strained his ears and held his breath, but all he could hear was Father William. 'Do they all have names?' he asked.

'Gran's given them names. Oh, Hal, they're like a proper family! There's William and Mary, that's the parents. The cubs are Winkin, Blinkin and Nod. Then there's Aunt May. She's got no babies of her own, but she used to baby-sit for Mary when they were little. Now she won't leave off. She's always fussing round them till Mary chases her away. So she goes off on her own and comes back carrying little prezzies for them in her mouth. Wriggly worms or crispy, crunchy beetles.'

'Just like our Aunt May,' grinned Hal.

'Come on,' said Ellie, 'we've got to finish tidying up.'

'My turn to shovel, then,' said Hal.

'OK. Let's get rid of this lot first, or we'll never be able to carry it.'

Between them they lugged the bag some distance from the sett, sprinkled the earth and trod it down and kicked dry leaves and twigs on top. Then they went back for a second load.

Something was still nagging away at the back of Hal's mind: a question that had to be asked. 'Ellie, why did you leave your shoes in the shed?'

'Tell you when we get home. Come on. Keep digging.'

As they were getting rid of the second load of earth, they heard Mum calling. Ellie grabbed Hal's hand and dived into the undergrowth, heading along another badger track which took them close enough to the road to force a way through. They crossed the road and climbed over the low garden wall, where the house hid them from Mum, who was standing at the kitchen door.

'Hal! Ellie!' she called again.

'Into the shrubbery!' hissed Ellie, dragging him

across the herb patch. Scents of thyme and marjoram and mint rose up around their feet, mingling with honeysuckle, rosemary, southernwood from the bushes surrounding them. Hal began to feel quite dizzy. As Mum came round the side of the house, Ellie stepped out of the shrubbery, still clutching Hal's hand.

'Where have you been?' asked Mum.

'In the shrubbery,' said Ellie innocently.

'What have you been doing?'

'Digging,' Hal improvised, suddenly realising he was still holding the trowel. Where Ellie had stashed the sack was anyone's guess.

'Didn't you hear me calling?'

'We thought you'd find us,' said Ellie, acting disappointed.

'Yes, well, I might have done, if you'd told me we were playing hide-and-seek. Come and get yourselves cleaned up. Then we can have some tea.'

Uncle Ho was back before them. He was sitting at the bottom of the garden, reporting back to Lemmy. At least, that was the way it looked, Lemmy leaning on his spade and Uncle Ho looking earnestly up at him.

* * *

As soon as they got home, Hal and Ellie went down to the shed at the bottom of the garden. There, tucked away behind the wheelbarrow, under a pile of sacks, stood Ellie's boots.

'That's why I left my trainers behind,' said Ellie. 'I changed into my boots.'

'Why didn't you wear your boots in the first place?'

'Smell them.'

Hal picked up the boots and sniffed them. Overlaying the smell of rubber was another scent. Warm and sort of hairy.

'Musk,' said Ellie proudly. 'Badger musk. It's like being made a blood-brother. It tells the rest of the tribe that you're an OK person. I didn't want Mum finding them and washing it off. I'd have had to start all over again. It took ages. Following them. Trying to keep downwind. Watching them digging for worms or grubbing up roots. Seeing the cubs playing up and down the bank and longing to pick them up and cuddle them, but Gran said I mustn't. I'd got to wait for them to come to me. Then one night, there was Mary, rubbing herself against my boots. I'm like one of the tribe now.'

'I wish —' Hal began. 'Do they only ever come out at night?'

'You want to see them?'

'I —'

'They go back to the sett when it starts getting light. I could take you then.'

'OK.'

'Tonight?'

Hal nodded. Better say yes, now. With Ellie, you might not get a second chance. You never knew where you were with Ellie. She could be as snappy as a terrier with toothache. Then again, she could be so NICE.

Five

The world at first light is a different place from the world of half an hour before or the world of half an hour after. It reminded Hal of being at the pantomime. In the darknesss the audience gradually falls silent, waiting for the curtain to rise.

There was none of that showy red-sky-in-the-morning business. Just a streak of white, spread across the inky-coloured sky, like a banner announcing the Greatest Show on Earth. Faint rustlings, like sweet papers in the misty half-light. The odd creak here and there, like someone getting settled in their seat. Then, finally, silence.

High above their heads, a solitary bird began to sing.

'Skylark,' said Gran briskly, hurrying on across the common. 'They're always the first to sing. Up there, it's dawn already. I'll have to leave you two by the badger sett. There's a car parked at the bottom of the lane and I want to know who it belongs to.'

Ellie could have warned him to wear his wellies. His jeans, from knee to ankle, were soon fit to be wrung out. Jogging the odd tree branch was like turning on a cold shower. By the time they reached the wood, Hal had decided he wasn't really a morning person after all.

'I'm just going to check on that car,' said Gran. 'If anyone comes, keep out of sight.'

Hal sat on the cold, hard ground, with dew-drops dripping down his neck and a spider trying to build a web between the hawthorn bush beside him and his ear.

'Stop fidgeting,' said Ellie.

'I can't help it. There's a bit of flint sticking into me.'

'Do you want to see badgers, or don't you?'

'I just wish we could see them from somewhere a bit more comfortable, that's all.'

'Boys are so soft!'

'Next time,' said Hal, 'I'll bring a cushion. And an umbrella.'

'Sh!' said Ellie. 'Listen!'

Hal listened. The air was gradually filling with noise. Birds tuning their voices ready for the dawn chorus. Scufflings and rustlings among the leaves, as the night shift of small creatures hurried home to sleep and the day shift got under way.

'Look!' whispered Ellie. 'Over there!'

Along the path they'd taken yesterday, coming from Gran's – the path for midgets, the path for dwarfs – a shadow moved. A pattern of shadows, coming closer.

'Father William,' whispered Ellie.

A white face, very thin. No: a white streak, with a dark streak either side, then another white one. See a picture of a badger and you'd think the markings would stand out a mile. But see a badger in the wild, dappled by light and shadow and those markings are perfect camouflage. If something had alarmed Father William now, all he had to do was stand stock-still and he would be invisible, even to Hal, who knew he was there.

Father William padded forward and stuck his head out into the clearing. He sniffed the morning air and found it good. He lifted up his head and listened to the sound of morning. That was good, too. He looked to left and right and back again. Then he made his way across the clearing towards the sett, confident that the day could be left to look after itself. He moved surprisingly quickly and smoothly, low to the ground, almost as if he was on wheels.

'What about the others?' Hal asked, when Father William had vanished underground.

'Mary and Aunt May are probably inside already. The cubs will be coming soon.'

It wasn't long before two little figures appeared on the path at the top of the bank, two Father Williams in miniature, who launched themselves over the edge and slid down on their tummies in a flurry of dust.

'I thought you said there were three?' whispered Hal.

'There are. Nod's the dozy one. Always last.'

Like two kids waiting for the rest of the gang to catch up, the cubs sat about for a bit. One of them scratched himself busily behind the ear with his back leg. The other yawned widely, then suddenly nipped the first one and dodged back and a mad chase began, round and round the clearing, first one, then the other in front, until they suddenly collided and began a mock fight, tangling and tumbling and pretending to bite.

'Someone's coming,' said Ellie suddenly.

Hal hadn't noticed, but now he could hear it. Voices. Stones kicked down the bank. Branches pushed back out of the way.

'Grab Winken,' Ellie ordered. 'I'll get Blinken.'

'What?' How was he supposed to know which was which?

Ellie grabbed one cub and dived for the cover of the bushes. Hal did his best with the other one and followed Ellie. The cub should have been grateful, but it wasn't. Needle-sharp teeth nipped his finger. The cub gave one thrust of its back legs and popped out of Hal's arms like a cork from a bottle and landed tumbling head over heels.

Winken – if it was Winken – was still getting his breath back when the terrier arrived on the scene. The dog gave a delighted bark and hurled itself at the badger cub, who fled for home, with the terrier yapping madly in pursuit. Straight down the nearest hole went Winken. Straight after him went the dog.

Seconds later, the yapping turned to a yelping and the dog shot out backwards almost as quickly as it had gone in, its nose a mass of blood. Just for a moment, Father William's head appeared at the entrance to the sett, with an expression that said quite clearly, 'And don't come back!' Then he was gone.

The terrier sat down and tried to lick its wounds, but its tongue wasn't long enough.

'Hey, Jude!' called a voice.

'Judy!'

Two men appeared on the path, with another dog, a lurcher, trailing behind them. One of the men – the shorter and fatter of the two – plainly fancied himself as Rambo. He'd tied a bandana round his head and ripped the sleeves out of his denim jacket. But the goose-pimples on his arms and his stomach hanging over the top of his combat trousers rather spoiled the effect.

The other one had modelled himself with more success on the Terminator, though the sunglasses were definitely a mistake at this time of day. He kept tripping over things.

Both of them carried guns. Rambo also carried a large flashlight and a brace of pheasants. The Terminator had his hands full of rabbits.

'Judy!' roared Rambo. 'Come 'ere!' Judy came 'ere. 'You come when I call you,' said Rambo, aiming a kick at her. He missed.

'What's done that to 'er, then?' enquired the other man.

'What?'

' 'Er nose.' He pushed his sunglasses up on top of his head so that he could see better. 'Fox, d'you reckon?'

'Fox!' Rambo was contemptuous. 'She don't go after foxes. She got more sense.' He stepped to the edge of the bank to get a closer look. The path crumbled under his weight so that he sat down suddenly and slid down into the clearing.

Rambo stood up, trying to look as if that was what he'd meant to do. 'Come and look at this,' he said.

The Terminator made his way down the slope, taking very small steps, like a ballet dancer, so as not to fall. After him and round him danced the lurcher.

'Well, what do you reckon?' demanded Rambo when his friend arrived at last. 'I reckon we got badgers,' he answered himself.

'Not many,' the other man observed. 'No more'n three entrances. Five of 'em. Six, maybe. Hardly worth the trouble.'

'Littl'uns fetch a few quid.'

'Road's close.'

'No cars, hardly.'

'What about the cottage, just across?'

'Just an old biddy on her own. What can she do?'

'Phone the Bill.'

'So we bring a few nets. We're after foxes. You did say you thought it was foxes.'

The big man smiled. 'Yeah.'

Not without some difficulty, the two of them scrambled back up the bank and disappeared down the path, followed by Judy. The lurcher lingered a bit longer, sniffing here, sniffing there. And that was the moment when Nod arrived at the top of the bank living in a little dreamworld of his own, chasing a butterfly – or perhaps it was a moth. Over the edge of the path he tumbled, head over heels all the way to the bottom, and came to a stop almost under the dog's nose.

The dog looked surprised. Nod looked dizzy. Well, thought the dog, it is about time for breakfast. Then something made him pause. He looked up, towards the other path, on the far side of the clearing, listening.

Hal heard it, too. A low growling that set the hackles rising on the back of his neck. The lurcher stood motionless, staring.

Among the shadows, through the leaves, Hal saw a face, narrow, pale grey, and the vague shape of a body behind it, poised to spring. There was power there, but controlled. The creature, whatever it was, would only attack if it had to. It went on staring out the lurcher until the dog finally turned and slunk away.

The cub, not one jot afraid, scuttled over to where the newcomer stood, still hidden amongst the leaves. For a moment Hal saw the grey head clearly as it bent and nuzzled the silly little creature. He must have made some sound. The narrow eyes flickered towards him, held him in their gaze. Then the creature turned and vanished in the shadows.

Nod was making for home.

Hal found he was shaking. 'Did you see it?' he asked Ellie.

'See what?' asked Ellie, putting Blinken down, so he could join the others.

'That – creature – that frightened the dog away.'

'One of the other badgers, I expect. They've probably got another entrance further along.'

'It didn't look . . . It looked more like . . .'

'What?'

'Nothing. I expect it was just a trick of the light.'

Then they heard Gran's voice, bright and clear, from further along the path. 'Good morning! It's going to be another lovely day, by the look of it!' He imagined her smiling at the two tough guys. 'Have you had good hunting? I see you have. Oh, your poor little dog! What happened to her nose? I've got some peroxide indoors, if you don't mind waiting while I fetch it.'

The men mumbled something.

'Oh, well,' came Gran's voice again, 'I daresay it's not as bad as it looks. Goodbye!'

Two minutes later, she joined Hal and Ellie in the clearing. 'They found them, then,' she said. 'At least, the little dog did. I know a badger bite when I see one. I suppose it was only a matter of time.'

'They won't gas them, will they, Gran?'

'I shouldn't think so, Hal. There's not so much of that nowadays. And this is common land. But there are other dangers. Badger baiting. They call it sport. It's gone on for centuries. I suppose there was some excuse for it in the old days, when people didn't understand that animals could feel pain.' Gran suddenly seemed very tired. She sat down on a fallen tree-trunk and she sighed. 'There was a sett the other side of Melford. Some men dug out the badgers and set their dogs on them. They killed seven adults and took the cubs away. Someone's keeping them somewhere. They use the little ones to train the dogs. I told Frank Finnegan all about it. I thought, if it was in the paper . . . but it wasn't.'

'I wouldn't like to be the dog that came up against Father William!' Hal declared.

'I'm afraid it's not as simple as that,' Gran said gently. 'The badger never wins. The odds are always stacked against him. Sometimes he's tethered to a stake, or imprisoned in a pipe so he can't retreat. Sometimes it's just a question of numbers, four or five dogs on to one. If the badger's still doing too well, the baiters wound him with knives or clubs, even break his legs. If he's a big, strong male, like Father William, they may pull out his teeth and claws before the fight ever begins.'

'What sort of people would do a thing like that?' whispered Hal.

Gran shrugged. 'Just ordinary people. They don't have horns and a tail or six-six-six stamped on their foreheads. Those two this morning, on the other hand . . . They may just be a couple of harmless poachers.'

'We heard them talking,' said Ellie. 'They don't *know* there are badgers. Not for sure.'

'One said something about it not being worth the trouble,' said Hal. 'Perhaps it'll be all right.'

'Tell the police,' suggested Ellie. 'Get them to lock them up.'

'They can't lock someone up,' said Gran, 'for something they might do. I wish I'd thought to take the number of the car. Anyway, time you two were back in bed. Come on.'

Outside the cover of the trees, morning had well and truly broken. The common was abuzz with activity, on the ground and in the trees, in the air above and in the earth under their feet as they hurried homewards.

As they reached the fence, Uncle Ho came high-stepping towards them through the wet grass. In the darkness of the night, he wouldn't have worried about getting his paws damp, but now the sun was turning him back into his daytime, comfort-loving self.

When Hal and Ellie were safely back inside the garden, Gran called softly, 'Ellie! I think it's better if you don't come again, until I know it's safe.'

'But, Gran!' Ellie protested.

'No buts, Ellie. We don't know who those people are.'

'But what about you, Gran?'

'I'll be safer on my own, without you to worry

about,' Gran said firmly. 'Now get to bed before your mother catches you – or you'll never be allowed out at night again.'

She strode away with Uncle Ho at her heels before Ellie could argue any more.

Alone in his room, unable to sleep, Hal tried to conjure up the scene in the clearing again. What was it he'd seen? He knew it wasn't a badger. It couldn't be a wolf. There were no wolves any more. Not in England. Yet those sad eyes haunted him. It was almost as if they knew him.

Each evening before he went to bed, he knelt at the window, watching the dark spreading over the common, but there was never a sign of the creature.

Six

'Hal!' From the depths of sleep, he recognised Ellie's voice, worried, urgent.

Hal opened his eyes. The room was pitch-black. What time was it? What day was it? Friday night, going on Saturday morning.

'Hal!' Hard little fingers gripped his shoulder and shook it.

'Gerroff,' muttered Hal.

'Hal! Wake up! Please, you've got to wake up. It's Gran!'

Hal sat up and switched on the light. 'What about Gran?'

Ellie stood by his bed fully dressed and filthy dirty, as if she'd been wrestling in mud. There were leaves and bits of twig in her hair and sweater and long, clean streaks on her face where she'd been crying.

'Ellie! What is it?'

'It's Gran!'

'What about Gran?'

'She's hurt,' whispered Ellie. 'She's lying in the clearing by the badger sett. I couldn't get her to wake up.'

'We'd better wake Dad.'

'You do it.' Just as he reached the door she suddenly called out, 'Hal! Don't tell him it was me that found her.'

He nodded. 'Right.'

He padded along the landing to his parents' room. 'Dad! Dad, wake up!'

'What is it?' Dad, bleary-eyed, making out Hal's figure standing over him in the dim light from the landing. A quick glance at Mum, who slept on, oblivious.

'It's Gran, Dad. I think she's had an accident.'

'What sort of accident?'

'I don't know. She's lying in the wood, just opposite the house.'

Dad stared at Hal's worried face in silence.

'Where the path across the common turns off through the wood,' said Hal. 'There's a bank sloping down towards the road. That's where she is, at the bottom of the bank.'

Hal waited for the question: 'How do you know?' All Dad said was, 'I'd better go and see.' Suddenly he was Action Man, wide awake, out of bed and pulling on his clothes.

'Better not wake Mum for the moment,' he said. 'Will you be all right? Looking after things here?'

Hal nodded.

'Right. Shan't be long.'

On the way back to his room, Hal looked in on Jack. Jack was wide awake. He stood, gripping the bars of his cot, gazing through a gap in the curtains at the clouds drifting across the moon. Hal drew back the curtains a bit more and left him to it. Downstairs, he heard the car start up and drive away.

When he got back to his own room, he found Ellie standing just as he had left her. 'Dad's gone to take a look,' he told her.

Ellie sank down on to the bed. 'You didn't tell him it was me that found her?'

'He didn't ask. I'm asking. What were you doing out there, after Gran told you not to go?'

'It was just as well I did go, wasn't it?' snapped Ellie. 'Or she might have been lying there till she was dead! *They* wouldn't have cared!'

'Sh! You'll wake Mum. Who's *they*? Who are you talking about? What did you see?'

She took a deep breath. 'I didn't see anything. I only heard. Voices. I was just going to take a little look. Just to make sure the cubs were all right. Then, before I got there, I heard voices. A man's voice. And Gran's.'

'What were they saying?'

'I can't remember. She sounded angry. And a bit scared. Then the man again.' She shook her head, frowning. 'No. Two men. They were all sort of talking together, and then . . . I heard Gran cry out. And they were shouting and the dogs were barking and I couldn't do anything. I thought any minute they'd be coming after me!'

'Did you see who it was?'

Ellie shook her head. 'I crawled into the bushes as far as I could. I waited and waited in case they came back. Then I went to see. There was a cut on her head and blood all over the place. She wouldn't wake up. And I got the feeling there was someone – something – still there, watching me. So I ran.' Ellie's eyes were wide and she was trembling from head to foot.

'Better get out of those clothes,' Hal said. 'They're filthy.'

Ellie did as she was told. He noticed she'd remembered out of habit to take off her boots. But she'd forgotten to put on her trainers. She must have run barefoot up the garden. He led her to the bathroom and washed her hands and feet. Bundling up her muddy clothes, he hid them away in the bottom of the wardrobe. Somehow he'd have to find a time to wash them when Mum wasn't about.

He tucked Ellie into his bed, which was still a bit warm. One thing he had to know. 'Why didn't you want me to tell Dad it was you that found Gran? I thought you said he knew about you going out at night?'

'I only asked him once,' said Ellie. 'I think he thought it was just the once. Don't tell him it was me, Hal. Please don't tell him. Or he won't let me go ever again.'

'I won't tell him,' said Hal.

'Promise?'

'I promise. Go to sleep now.'

'What will you tell him?' enquired Ellie drowsily.

'I'll think of something.'

He did try to think of something. Sitting by the

window, while Ellie slept, watching the dawn come up, he did try.

It was a different kind of dawn from the last one he'd seen. As the sun's rays warmed the earth, threads of mist appeared out of nowhere and formed themselves into clouds, reminding him of something he'd seen once on the telly about the birth of stars. From the direction of Gran's house he thought he heard a motor. Not a car. An ambulance? Dad would have called the ambulance. Would he go with it to the hospital? Or come straight back, start asking questions?

What could he say, without telling a lie, that wouldn't get Ellie into trouble? The best thing he could come up with was the Code of the Stittles: *say nothing*.

At last he heard the car come back; heard the back door open and close; Dad coming up the stairs. Hal went out on to the landing. 'Is Gran all right?' he whispered.

'She was still unconscious when the ambulance arrived. They think she'll be OK. It would have been a different story if she'd lain there till morning, or even longer. There can't be many people who go that way. Hal, how did you know she was there?'

Say nothing. 'I just knew.'

'Were you out there yourself?'

Hal shook his head.

'You can tell me. I won't be angry. You probably saved Gran's life.'

'I'd never go out in the dark. You know that.'

'But it wasn't *that* dark, was it?' Dad persisted gently.

'What's going on?' demanded Ellie's voice. She came along the landing, rubbing the sleep from her eyes. She was wearing Hal's dressing-gown, but if Dad noticed this, he didn't say so. 'Why are you out here whispering?' she asked.

'So as not to wake anyone,' whispered Hal.

'Well, you've woken me.'

'Yes, well, let's not wake Mum yet,' said Dad.

'What's going on?'

'Your gran's been taken to hospital.'

'Is she ill?'

'She had – a slight accident – while she was out walking last night.'

'Oh, poor Gran! Is it bad?'

'It would have been much worse if Hal hadn't raised the alarm.' Dad looked from Hal to Ellie and back again. 'He's quite a hero. You'd better get back to bed, Ellie. You're shivering with cold. I'll go and make us a cup of tea before I wake Mum and tell her.'

Hal went to check on Jack again. As the moon went down and the sun came up, Jack had lost interest in the Wonderful World of Nature. He was fast asleep, on all fours, with his bottom sticking up in the air. Hal tucked the covers round him as best he could. Coming out on to the landing, he heard voices from Mum and Dad's room, too quiet for him to make out what they were saying. Dad came out with Ellie's cup of tea and winked at him in passing.

After breakfast, Dad went over to Gran's to feed the chickens and make sure everything was locked up and switched off. When he came back, he brought Uncle Ho with him, glaring through the mesh of the cage Gran used for taking him to the vet's.

'Take him through to the garden,' said Mum, 'before you let him out.'

'Stand back,' said Dad, as he opened the flap. 'He's not in a very good mood.'

Uncle Ho emerged slowly, swishing his tail. He yawned. He sniffed the air. He stalked to one side of the garden, and back again to the other. Then with an air of 'been there, done that, got the T-shirt', he climbed back into the cage and sat waiting for someone to take him home.

He was still sitting there when Mum, Dad, Hal and Ellie left for the hospital to visit Gran, after getting Mrs Next-Door in to look after Jack.

Dad had to stop the car four times on the way, for Mum to buy grapes, women's magazines, a bunch of carnations and a get-well card.

They arrived at last at the hospital and found the little room where Gran lay all alone. It was painted in that shade of hospital green that makes you feel ill, just to look at it. Hal and Ellie peeped through the porthole in the door and saw Gran propped up in bed, looking very small and frail. Her skin was ashy-grey. There was a dressing over one eye, held in place by a bandage wound round her head. One arm was in a sling. The other had a drip-feed leading from it. Her head was turned towards the door, but she didn't seem to see them, even when Hal pressed his nose up against the glass and grinned at her.

The doctor took Mum and Dad to one side, speaking in a low voice, 'Your mother – it is your mother?' Dad nodded. 'She's lucky she's got such a thick skull. It's just a hairline fracture. No permanent damage. The eye looks a lot worse than it is. A cut there always bleeds a lot, but it's just four stitches and a shiner any boxer would be proud of. Her wrist is badly sprained, but not broken. Apart from that, it's just a few cracked ribs. I think the two of you should go in alone,' he said. 'Leave the kids outside.'

'Please can't we see her too?' begged Ellie, giving him her sweetest smile. 'We'll be good.'

'Your turn tomorrow,' said the doctor.

'Why not till then?' Ellie pouted.

'Because I say so.' He grinned. 'And I'm in charge.' He turned to Mum and Dad. 'I'll come in with you for a moment. Don't worry if she seems a bit vague. We've got her drugged up to the eyeballs with painkillers and tranquillisers. I suppose you don't happen to know what she normally takes? For her arthritis and so on?'

'She never takes anything,' said Dad. 'Not even aspirin.'

'Good grief. Well, that gives us a clear field, doesn't it?'

Hal and Ellie found themselves seats in the waiting area. There were plenty to choose from. The only other person there was a young man with a

96

ponytail, dressed in jeans and a trench coat, who was leaning against the wall with his hands in his pockets. As the doctor came out of Gran's room, he pushed himself off from the wall and came to a stop blocking the doctor's way.

'She's OK to receive visitors, then,' he said.

'Family only,' said the doctor.

'All I want is a few words. Did she fall or was she pushed?'

'I can't say.'

'Gimme a break, Ben. I'm due off at twelve, but I've got to get a report in before the old man will let me go.'

'Sorry.'

'But I've got tickets for the match this afternoon.'

'Lucky you! This time tomorrow, I'll still be on call. Excuse me. I'm wanted in Casualty.'

As Dr Ben brushed past him, the young man glanced towards the door of Gran's room.

'Don't even *think* of it, Kit,' said Dr Ben. The young man muttered something under his breath as the doctor strode off down the corridor, but he was smiling as he turned back to Hal and Ellie and sat himself down facing them.

'Your gran, is it?' he asked. 'In there?'

'No comment,' said Ellie swiftly. 'Are you a reporter?'

He shook his head. His smile broadened. 'No. Police.'

'Where's your ID, then?'

He took a small plastic holder from his pocket and flipped it open to show a photograph. 'DC Marlowe. Satisfied?'

Ellie still looked suspicious.

DC Marlowe kept smiling. 'Call me Kit. Everyone does. What's your name?'

'Eleanor May Cornish,' said Ellie. 'That's my brother Hal.'

Kit nodded pleasantly at Hal. 'So,' he said, 'which of you two angels was it who raised the alarm?'

Hal looked to Ellie for guidance.

'No comment,' said Ellie again.

'What about you, Hal?'

Hal sat, staring at his shoes. *Say nothing.*

'He can talk, can he?' said Kit to Ellie.

'Of course I can talk,' said Hal. 'When I want to.'

'Well, then, which one of you was it? There's no need to be frightened. Your gran will tell us what happened when she's feeling better. Look, when there's a nine-nine-nine call in the middle of the night, we generally send a car, just in case. A man was seen running away, so we picked him up. If you say he had nothing to do with what happened to your gran, we can eliminate him from our enquiries. So just tell me what you saw.'

'Nothing,' mumbled Hal.

'Sorry? I didn't catch that.'

'He didn't see anything,' said Ellie. 'Neither did I. Neither of us saw anything.'

'What was it you heard, then?'

Ellie looked mutinous.

Hal stared at the floor.

'Was it someone you know?'

Ellie frowned. She got up and went to the door of Gran's room and knocked.

Dad stuck his head out. 'What is it, Ellie?'

'This man won't stop talking to us,' said Ellie.

Kit Marlowe already had his ID out and was waving it like a magic talisman. 'Police,' he said. 'We were just chatting.'

Dad looked him up and down. 'If you want to interview my children, you'd better arrange a proper time and place, so that I can be there with them.'

'Fair enough, sir. We think we've got the right man, but we need to be sure. Since Mrs Cornish isn't 'fit to make a statement yet . . .'

'He just wants to get to his football match,' said Ellie.

'Cricket,' Kit corrected her affably. 'Thanks, kids. You've been a great help.'

'But we didn't tell you anything,' said Hal.

The policeman grinned. 'That's what's interesting. I daresay it will do to be going on with.'

As they were driving home, Mum said, 'I wonder if we should send for Aunt May?'

'That might be difficult,' said Dad. 'Last time I heard, she was halfway up the Nile. I'll leave a message for when she comes home.'

'All the same, it might be important.'

'Mum's not that bad. It'll keep.'

'But she did mention Aunt May. Several times.'

'She also talked about Winken, Blinken and Nod. Any ideas about getting in touch with them?'

When they got home, Uncle Ho had next-door's cat marooned on top of the garden shed. Every time it moved to a different part of the roof, hoping to jump down and escape, Uncle Ho was there before it. Mrs Next-Door was putting down saucers of milk, trying to lure him away and Jack was following her round, emptying the saucers down his front as he tried to drink from them.

Dad had to climb up the stepladder and lure the terrified trespasser into Uncle Ho's travelling-cage. Uncle Ho wasn't using it any more. By the time all the fuss was over, he was long gone.

Seven

Next morning, Uncle Ho hadn't returned.

Mum was worried. 'He'll be hungry,' she said, forking cat food and pouring milk into the two halves of the dish Dad had brought home for him.

'If he's really hungry,' said Ellie, 'then he'll come. He knows the way.'

Mum stood at the back door with the dish in her hand. 'Kitty, kitty, kitty!' she called.

Next-door's cat appeared on top of the fence. It looked hopeful, then embarrassed, and disappeared again.

'Just leave it there,' said Ellie.

'I can't do that,' she said. 'Jack might get at it.'

'What if I put it the other side of the fence?' suggested Hal.

'Thank you, Hal.' Mum handed him the dish and went back indoors.

Being careful not to spill the milk, Hal climbed up the rockery and over the chain-link fence. He put down the dish and looked around. He had the strong impression that Uncle Ho wasn't far away. But which way?

Hal closed his eyes, listening. He felt the breeze on his cheek, and on the other side of him a rustling that was not the breeze. 'Uncle Ho?'

He had a definite feeling that he wasn't alone, but now the movement came from behind him. He turned.

Suddenly a thick brown-paper sack was flung over his head, a rope fastened round it, pinioning his arms, and he was knocked off his feet onto a hard wooden surface and being carried away at bone-cracking speed. He tried to cry out, but as soon as he took a breath his throat was filled with dust that smelled of chicken-feed and all he could do was cough, while the cart trundled on, away from home and safety.

A cart. Low-down. Four wheels. A go-cart, probably.

Every now and then, there would be a jolt and he

and the cart would part company. A hand would shove him roughly back on again. Not a grown-up's hand. Stittles! thought Hal. Stittles. He was sure of it, long before that juddering, shuddering ride came to a sudden stop and he was tipped out on to the bare earth.

There was a muttering and arguing in low voices. Then everything went quiet, apart from a sinister metallic rustling somewhere above him. Someone untied the rope and took the bag off his head. Hal found himself crouching on the ground under the tree where the dead things hung.

Below it, on a log, sat Rutger Stittle, wearing a Home Guard helmet, a moth-eaten fur coat draped round his shoulders, with the sleeves turned inside to make a cloak. Beside him on the ground crouched Michelle, looking like Dracula's sister, pure Gothic, apart from the wreath of wild flowers on her head. The other Stittles clustered around: Harrison, Dustin, Dolph and Madonna. Above, in the Hanging Tree, crouched Uncle Ho.

'Traitor!' Hal hissed at him. Uncle Ho swung his tail.

'Traitor!' exclaimed Rutger. 'That's good, that is. That's really good, comin' from you!'

'Me?' said Hal. 'What am I supposed to have done?'

'What have you done?' repeated Rutger. 'We'll show you what you done! Prepare him!' he ordered.

The twins grabbed hold of Hal. They streaked his face with mud and rubbed ashes in his hair. Hal stopped struggling as soon as he realised they'd done the same to themselves.

'Come on,' said Rutger.

They set off in single file across the common. Michelle led the way, crooning softly to herself. Nobody else made any noise, except Dolph, when Madonna let a bramble swing back and it scratched him just above the eye. After Michelle marched Rutger, hands at his sides, tight-clenched. Hal was sandwiched between the twins. Madonna and Dolph brought up the rear.

Hal kept looking round, thinking rescue couldn't be far away. It was Sunday morning, for heaven's sake. People ought to be out jogging, walking their dogs, or taking the pretty way to church. But when people see a bunch of kids in the middle of a serious game, they tend to give them a wide berth. Especially when they're the Stittles.

They stopped beside a newly dug pit, with a pile

of earth beside it. Someone shoved him forward until he was teetering on the edge. He looked down automatically, to see how far he had to fall, and saw something lying at the bottom. At first he took it for another old fur coat, dusty and crawling with flies. Then he saw that where the flies were, there were patches of blood. Then he could make out the shape of the snout, the head, the paws and the unmistakable markings of a badger.

Dead. Aunt May? Probably. Off on her own, in search of new and exciting titbits for the young ones.

'We just wanted you to see,' said Rutger. 'We just wanted to show you what you done.'

'What *I*'ve done?' said Hal. 'What's it got to do with me?'

'Let the ceremony commence,' said Michelle.

For one panic-filled moment, Hal thought they were going to push him in and bury him along with the badger. Then Dustin and Harrison grabbed his arms and hauled him back. Softly Michelle began to sing again. This time Hal recognised the tune: 'Amazing Grace'. It sounded really good.

While she was singing, Rutger stepped forward, lifting up his arms. 'Ashes to ashes,' he chanted. 'Dust to dust,' opening his clenched fists, to scatter dust from one and ashes from the other.

'Rest in peace,' said Dustin, holding up a dead mouse by the tail before dropping it into the grave.

'Cheers,' said Harrison, tossing in a half-empty can of Coke.

Dolph's offering was a sprinkling of old Mr Stittle's herbal mixture. 'RSVP,' he muttered.

'RIP,' Rutger corrected him, out of the corner of his mouth.

Madonna pulled off her hair ribbon, kissed it and threw it in with the rest.

They all looked at Hal, who was feeling feverishly in his pockets for something suitable. Library ticket? Pen? Bit of string? Chewing-gum? At last he produced an almost-new packet of peppermints. Rutger nodded: peppermints were OK. Hal threw them in.

That left Michelle. She finished her song, took off her crown of flowers and tossed it into the grave, saying, 'Sweets to the sweet. Farewell!'

They got that out of a film, thought Hal. Not one film – lots of films. Mrs Stittle was a great film fan, always down at the video shop.

Then he stood transfixed as the Stittle voices rose together in a weird, trembling cry that went on and on. It was a sound to make your hair stand on end and the soles of your feet tingle, as if it was travelling deep underground as well as through the air, beyond the far horizon. Hal could imagine distant dogs joining in and cats bolting up trees, for no reason that their owners could see or hear.

Then suddenly it stopped.

Rutger said, 'Peace! The charm's wound up.' From somewhere he produced a garden spade and handed it to Hal. 'Fill it in,' he ordered.

Hal did as he was told, while the Stittles stood and watched in silence. He got the feeling they were all thinking they could do it better, but not one of them offered to help.

He was feeling more indignant than frightened by the time they led him back to the Hanging Tree. Before the Stittles had sorted themselves out – while Rutger was trying to shift Dolph's foot off his robe, so that he could seat himself on his throne again – 'Look,' said Hal, 'one of the badgers is dead –'

'Murdered,' put in Dolph.

'Murdered, even,' said Hal. 'And I'm really, really sorry. But it's not my fault.'

' 'Tis,' said Dolph.

Rutger gave an extra hard tug at his robe and Dolph fell over. Rutger sat down. 'You dobbed in Lemmy,' he said.

'I didn't,' said Hal, frowning, but the words were lost, as all the Stittles started talking at once.

'They said he done it and he never did!'

'He never hit no one!'

'Lemmy was lookin' after 'em.'

'It never would of happened if Lemmy had been there!'

'It's your fault!'

'Grassin' on our Lemmy when he never done nothin'.'

'You're a grass an' a liar.'

'An effin' liar!'

'Shut up!' roared Hal, so loudly, he surprised himself. But it was the kind of language the Stittles understood. They shut up. Hal took a deep breath. 'You're saying the police have arrested Lemmy. Is that right?'

The Stittles all opened their mouths to answer. 'One at a time,' Hal told them. 'Rutger?'

'That's right,' said Rutger belligerently.

'Don't tell us you didn't know,' put in Dolph. Rutger glared at him.

'I didn't,' said Hal. 'What have they arrested him for?'

'For duffin' up your gran. And he never. They came round to the house yesterday morning and took him away. They said he'd been seen. They said they got a witness. That's gotta be you 'cos it was you that got your dad to call the amb'lance.'

'How did you know that?'

'We got our sources.'

'I just knew she was in trouble,' said Hal. 'I wasn't there. I didn't see anything. I just sort of knew. Understand?'

Curiously enough, the Stittles did seem to understand.

'But I think the police have made a mistake. As soon as they find out, they'll let him go.'

'You tell 'em,' said Rutger.

'They gotta let him out today, right?'

'Right.'

'He can't stand being locked up,' said Dolph.

'Shut up,' said Rutger.

'Have you checked on the other badgers?' asked Hal. 'Are they all right?'

The Stittles looked at one another.

'We woulda done.'

'If we knew where.'

'Lemmy never told us.'

'We never asked him.'

'It's best that way.'

They all suddenly stopped talking and glanced at one another or stared into the distance over Hal's shoulder.

'It's just as well I know, then,' said Hal. 'Come on.'

He set off across the common with the Stittles trailing behind him. It felt weird, him leading the Stittles gang, like some old explorer. For the moment, the natives trusted him, but one false move . . .

He just hoped he could lead them to the right place. There was a hundred-metre stretch where the path ran through the wood and a good fifty metres was along the top of the bank, where grass and brambles hid most of the ground below. Where the sett was, he remembered, the bank jutted out, giving extra cover.

At least, it used to. Above where the sett had been, both bank and path had crumbled away. Hal scrambled down into the clearing which had been so peaceful before, layers of dead leaves lying undisturbed, year after year. Now it looked as if a hurricane had hit it, with the leaves scuffed up into grubby heaps and the bare earth beneath pitted and scratched. Hal stood staring in disbelief at where the main entrance to the sett had been dug out, or caved in.

The Stittles, without a word of command, fanned out like Indian trackers, examining scuff marks and bootprints and signs of something heavy being dragged away. They fingered broken branches, tufts of hair and scattered drops of blood and checked out the other two entrances, both blocked with stones and clay and bits of barbed wire. Then they gathered again round Hal to compare notes.

Last came the twins, wriggling on their tummies from under a thicket of hawthorn and brambles. 'We found the bolthole the dead 'un used,' reported Dustin. 'No more in there.'

'She put up a real old fight, she did, before she made a run for it.'

'Somebody's dog won't be feeling too clever,' said Harrison with satisfaction.

'No more dead?' asked Rutger.

'No.'

'They took 'em all, then. Good.'

'What's good about it?' demanded Hal.

'It gives us a chance to find 'em, right? Sometimes,' he explained, 'you get a whole gang with dogs. They dig 'em out and they set the dogs on them and kill 'em right there.'

'Too close to the road for that,' observed Dolph.

'How many do you reckon?' asked Rutger.

No more than three men, was the opinion. Maybe just two.

'I think I know who it might be,' said Hal. 'We saw two poachers. They knew the badgers were here. If it's not them they might have told somebody else . . .' Quickly he told them all he knew about Rambo and the Terminator.

'Listen!' said Dolph suddenly, holding up his hand for silence.

They listened. Birdsong. Rustling of the wind in the upper branches. And the sound of somebody quietly sobbing. It came from the badger track that led towards Gran's cottage. Rutger made a move towards it, but, 'Let me,' said Hal. 'I think I know who it is.'

Crouching double, he made his way along the path until he came to the place where Ellie sat, cradling one of the badger cubs in her arms. 'Ellie,' he whispered. 'It's all right, Ellie. It's me. Hal. Are you all right?'

Ellie choked back another sob and nodded.

'Who is it you've got there? Is it Nod?' A good guess. Ellie nodded again. 'How is he?'

Ellie held out the little badger, so that Hal could see the wound on its neck, and the small chest breathing deeply, in and out, like silent sobbing.

'He's hurt, Hal,' she whispered.

'Bring him out, then. We can't do him any good just sitting in here. Do you want me to take him?'

Ellie shook her head.

Hal moved slowly backwards out of the tunnel, ready to catch Ellie as she half-crawled, half-stumbled after him. At last they reached the clearing again. Ellie frowned when she saw the Stittles.

'It's all right, Ellie. They're with us.'

Ellie turned back to Nod. 'If Gran was here,' she said, 'she'd put some stuff on it to make it better. The stuff she put on Uncle Ho's paw when he got caught in the barbed wire.'

'You know where she keeps it?' demanded Rutger.

'Yes,' said Ellie. 'But we can't get in.'

'Trust me,' said Rutger. He led the way through the bushes, where the badger-nappers had opened up a path you could have cycled through, then down the road.

Outside the front door he paused, surveying the old-fashioned keyhole and the smart new Yale lock Mum had had put in. 'She use one or both?' asked Rutger.

'Just the Yale,' said Hal. 'She lost the key to the other one years ago.' Mum had nearly had a fit when she heard Gran never locked the door when she went out. 'There are bolts as well,' he added. 'Top and bottom.'

Rutger smiled, as if Hal were a backward five-year-old. 'You can't fasten bolts from the outside. It's just the key we need. Where does she keep the spare?'

'What spare?'

'People who live on their own, they always keep a spare key somewhere, in case they lock themselves out, right?'

Hal shrugged. 'I don't know.'

'Start looking,' Rutger told the others.

The Stittles fanned out and began to search methodically. It was worrying to see how efficiently they went about it, beginning with the porch and working outwards. They felt above the door and under the mat. They groped inside the cat-flap. They tipped up Gran's boots and the watering-can. They lifted flowerpots, loose bricks and paving stones and groped inside the window-boxes.

'Shed's locked,' reported Dolph.

'Try the chicken house,' ordered Rutger. 'I'm goin' to take a look around.'

Angry squawks came from the chicken house as the twins invaded. Two of the chickens, in a panic, fluttered to the top of the wire fence and sat teetering between home and freedom. The twins came out again empty-handed, leaving the girls to shoo the chickens back in. Wherever Gran hid her spare key – if she had one – she seemed to be a lot smarter than the Stittles.

A shout came from Rutger at the back of the house and Hal remembered the fanlight on the downstairs loo. You never could shut it properly, but the gap was so small, it hardly mattered, Gran said. Rutger already had it prised open. 'Donna,' he called. 'Dolph.'

Dolph stood under the window and made a stirrup with his hands. Madonna put her foot in it and he hoisted her up. She wriggled her head and one arm through the window, while Dolph held her feet. They heard the lid of the toilet seat crash down. Then Madonna gave a little wiggle and the rest of her disappeared inside. By the time they got round to the front door again, Madonna had it open. The Stittles poured inside like an invading army.

'Stay where I can see you, OK?' said Hal.

Rutger grinned at him. 'That's a nice way to ask visitors in, that is.'

'Sorry,' mumbled Hal.

' 'Sall right,' said Rutger, patting him on the shoulder. 'We got a reputation to keep up. But she's all right, your gran. We wouldn't nick nothing off your gran.'

'Our mum'd knock us into the middle of next week if we did,' put in Dolph.

'Where's this med'cine, then?' demanded Michelle.

'In the larder,' said Ellie. She still held tight to little Nod, but she seemed to be feeling better now that something was happening.

Gran's medicine store would not have disgraced your average witch. There were bundles of leaves strung up to dry and pots of creams and strange-smelling powders. Bottles in clear glass, or green, or blue, with handwritten labels.

'It was in a bottle,' said Ellie. 'I don't remember the name of it. Read them out.'

'Witch hazel?' suggested Hal. 'Glycerine?

Elderflower lotion? No, that's for eyes. Pot. permanganate?'

To each of these Ellie shook her head.

'Rose water? Hydrogen peroxide?'

'Wait!' Ellie frowned. 'That *might* be it.'

Michelle uncorked the bottle and sniffed. 'Smells like the stuff Mia puts on her hair. Can't do no harm, I s'pose.'

'Peroxide,' said Hal, remembering Gran talking to the two men after the little dog, Judy, got hurt. 'Peroxide. That's it.'

'Cotton wool?' demanded Michelle.

There was no cotton wool. Hal tore a piece off an old sheet that Gran was using for dusters. Back in the kitchen, Ellie held Nod, while Michelle cleaned the cut. As soon as she touched him, the cub wriggled and made little noises of protest.

'Water's cold, I expect,' said Michelle. She smiled. 'Shows he's not hurt so bad after all. Just frightened, mostly.'

Nod's claws were digging into Ellie's arm, but she didn't cry out or flinch, while Michelle worked away. 'Got any scissors?' she asked.

Hal found Gran's sewing scissors and Michelle clipped away the matted fur.

Madonna was tugging out Uncle Ho's basket from its corner by the stove. 'We gotta put him to bed after,' she puffed. 'So's he can get better.'

Uncle Ho had wandered off for the moment, but he'd be back, wanting to know: 'Who's been sleeping in my bed?' Hal still wasn't sure where he stood with Madonna, so: 'Let's make him a bed of his own, shall we?' he suggested. 'With a hot-water bottle and everything?'

'All right,' said Madonna. 'I'll put the kettle on.'

Hal resisted the temptation to say things like, 'Are you sure you can manage?' and 'Be careful with the hot water.' He didn't want to be sat on again. Upstairs he found Gran's rubber hot-water bottle. He took an oldish-looking towel from the airing cupboard and one of the top drawers from the tallboy in the spare bedroom.

Soon Nod was tucked up in his new bed in the middle of the kitchen floor. They sat around watching for signs of improvement. If wishing could have made him better, he'd have been on his feet again by now, but he just lay there, looking dozy.

Dolph rolled himself a cigarette, lit it and took a puff, then passed it on to Dustin, who was nearest. Dustin puffed at it, then passed it on. Hal watched uneasily as it came nearer. It smelt like old socks, but Ellie took a puff without keeling over. Hal took his turn and decided that the best thing about smoking was the lungful of clean air you enjoyed afterwards. He was relieved to see that when the cigarette got back to Dolph again, it stayed there.

He was beginning to feel hungry. Gran's clock was stopped as usual at five past seven, but it must be nearly dinner-time. Mum would be wondering where they were. The Stittles showed no sign of breaking up the party.

He glanced at Ellie. She was piggy-eyed and puddingy with crying and lack of sleep. This was no time to tell her about Lemmy's arrest. No time to ask her if he could possibly have been one of the two men she heard. Lemmy? No! Lemmy wouldn't hurt a caterpillar.

There was the sound of a car stopping outside. Footsteps on the gravel. Nobody moved. It was impossible to see in through the net curtain on the window, so long as nobody moved . . .

The footsteps went on, past the porch. Stopped. And started making their way back.

At the sound of the key turning in the lock, the Stittles, as one man, bolted for cover, into cupboards and behind furniture. Madonna burrowed under the cushions and the knitted shawl that covered the couch.

Hal found himself in the larder, peeping through the crack by the door-hinge, as the kitchen door opened. He could see the sleeve of a man's tweed jacket. Not police. He felt the Stittles' relief. The man came further into the room, and stopped when he saw Nod lying in his little bed. He bent down to look closer.

Hal decided it was time to put in an appearance. 'Hello, Dad,' he said.

Dad reacted surprisingly well as Stittles tumbled out on all sides, like an Apache ambush. 'Hello,' he said. 'Fancy meeting you here.

'Remind me to fix that window,' he said, when the Stittles had all stopped talking at once and Hal had explained how they got in and why.

Dad knelt down to look at little Nod again, without touching him. 'You ought to take him to the vet,' he said.

'No!' said Michelle.

'He might be hurt inside. You can't leave him here.'

'We're taking him to me grandad,' said Rutger. 'He'll know what to do.'

'I think he'll say the same as me.'

'He won't,' said Dolph darkly.

Dolph was probably right. Old Mr Stittle dismissed all modern medicine as a load of expensive mumbo-jumbo. 'Common sense, boy,' he declared, 'that's all you need, is common sense.' The vet, on his side, would have liked to know what moonlight and funny mushrooms and bits of red thread tied in odd places had to do with common sense, but nobody could tell him, least of all Mr Stittle.

The Stittles departed, taking little Nod with them.

'Home, then,' said Dad. 'I'd better tell Mum you've been with me, OK?'

Eight

When Mum sent him upstairs to get ready for
visiting Gran in the hospital, Hal found Ellie
sprawled across her bed, sound asleep.

'Leave her,' said Dad. 'She can visit Gran tomorrow.'

Mum was staying home anyway, to look after Jack.
She didn't want to bother Mrs Next-Door again.

As Dad turned the car into the stream of traffic
bound for Melford, Hal said, 'Dad . . .'

'Yes?' said Dad, eyes on the road.

'Nothing.'

Dad, still watching the traffic, said casually, 'It was
Ellie who raised the alarm, wasn't it?'

Hal nodded.

'Then she swore you to secrecy, right?'

'How did you know?'

'I guessed.'

Gran lay just as she had the day before, except that someone had taken away the drip-feed and tidied Mum's magazines into a neat pile on the bedside cabinet. They didn't look as if they had been opened.

'Hello, Gran,' said Hal.

Gran smiled, in a dreamy kind of way. 'Oh!' she said, when at last she recognised him. 'Is it Saturday?' Then she slowly took in her surroundings, the awful green paint and the hospital furniture. 'Oh,' she said again, disappointed.

Hal tried to sound cheerful. 'How are you feeling, Gran?'

She frowned, considering. 'I'm not sure. They've given me so many pills and things. Pills to make me sleep. Pills to wake me up. Pills for my heart and my arthritis . . . One day,' she said crossly, 'they'll invent a pill to make us live for ever. And then . . . And then . . .' Her voice trailed away again.

To cheer her up, Dad told her about Uncle Ho terrorising next-door's cat. Any other time, Gran would have laughed and laughed. But her mind was wandering far away. It took her a long while to drag it back before she smiled politely and said, 'Did he really, dear?' So Dad turned to more everyday things. He'd let out the Aga and emptied the fridge and he was going to make sure the house was aired every day when he went over to feed the chickens.

'Oh, Lemmy can do that, dear. Ask Lemmy to feed the chickens and give him a key, so that he can ... That is something you can do.' She paused, trying to collect her thoughts, which seemed to be wandering off again without her permission. 'On your way home, call in at the Stittles. Tell Lemmy ... Better still, tell Mia. She'll make sure he gets it right. Tell them they can have the eggs and any vegetables ... there'll be potatoes, and some peas, and ... no, that's not right. You'll be wanting some, too. Tell him ... Tell him ...' Then she lost the track completely. She seemed about to cry, fumbled for the tissues. 'Just give me a moment. I'll be all right.'

'I'll see to everything, Mum, don't worry.'

Hal beckoned Dad away from the bed. 'Was she talking about Lemmy when they took her to the ambulance?' he whispered. That would explain it: why they'd arrested him, said they'd got a witness.

Dad looked puzzled. He shook his head. 'She was unconscious. Why?'

'The police think it was Lemmy who attacked her.'

125

'Lemmy?' Though he spoke softly, Gran heard him. 'They think Lemmy attacked me? Lemmy Stittle?' Her face broke into a smile and she began to chuckle. 'Oh, don't make me laugh. It hurts!'

'They've arrested him, Gran.'

Her laughter died away. 'Locked him up? They mustn't do that. Oh, poor Lemmy! Where's that policeman? I'll soon put him right.' She was pushing the clothes off, trying to scramble out of bed.

Dad covered her up again. 'He's gone, Mum. Won't be back until tomorrow. You can put it right then. You can tell him.'

'Tomorrow won't do! I'll phone him. Where's the phone? Let me go, Dan. I'm your mother!' In her struggles to get up, she flung out an arm and the jug of water on the bedside cabinet crashed to the floor.

A nurse came bustling in, as if she'd been lurking right outside, expecting something like this to happen. 'Time for your medicine, Mrs Cornish. Dear, dear, dear! What have we been up to? What have you been saying to her? Mrs Cornish, I want you back in bed this minute. And you two, OUT!'

She shooed them into the waiting area and there they sat while the glass and water were cleared up and Gran was tucked up in her bed again and given

126

a little something to calm her down. They were allowed back in to say their goodbyes, with the nurse standing by like a prison guard.

Gran was already drifting off to sleep, but her mind was still fixed on poor Lemmy. She clutched at Dad's sleeve. 'I've been in a police cell, Dan. I know what it's like. You mustn't let them keep Lemmy there another night. Promise me, Dan.'

'I promise. What did happen, Mum?'

'I can't honestly say I remember. But if it comes to court, I shall say the bank gave way and I just fell. So they might as well let Lemmy go. Make sure he keeps that promise, Hal.'

'I will, Gran. Goodbye, Gran. See you again soon?'

Gran's eyes were closed. There was no reply.

Ellie was up again when they got home. As the car turned into the drive, Hal saw her face at the window, bleary-eyed and grumpy. Before they were properly in the door, she started complaining. 'You went without me!'

'You were asleep,' said Hal.

'I wasn't. I was just resting. With my eyes closed.' She looked out of the window at the sound of the car starting up again. 'Where's Dad going?'

'He's going to get Lemmy out of jail.'

'What's Lemmy in jail for?'

'The police think he attacked Gran.'

'That's stupid.' She picked up the remote control of the telly and began to fiddle with it.

'You've got to tell them, Ellie. You've got to tell them what you saw.'

'I didn't see anything.'

'Heard, then.'

'Gran can tell them, can't she?'

'I'm not sure she remembers. She says she fell.'

'Perhaps she did.'

'Even if she did, those men walked away, leaving her unconscious. Why don't you talk to Dad? Tell him everything you can remember? He knows already it was you that found her.'

'I *knew* I couldn't trust you. Blabbermouth!'

'*I* didn't tell him. Dad's not stupid. He knows I wouldn't have gone out there. It had to be you.'

Ellie bit her lip and flipped a couple of channels. 'I don't want to talk about it.'

'Why not?'

'I can't. I just can't! OK?' She turned away and picked up a cushion to cuddle. Hal left her watching a fat man in a tartan jacket singing 'Bless This

House' to a lot of nuns. They were trying hard to look as if they were enjoying it.

When Dad came back from the police station, he almost tripped over Hal lurking just inside the door.

'It's all right,' he grinned. 'They're letting Lemmy go. I think they would have done anyway. They've got no good reason to hold him. It seems they took a look round after the ambulance had gone and saw Lemmy trying to sneak away through the bushes. Blood on his hands. Not his. They just wanted to ask him a few questions, but he bolted like a frightened rabbit. So they went round to the house and picked him up when he got there. Took him down to the nick so they could talk to him without a chorus of Stittles. All he had to tell them was how long he'd been there, whether he'd seen anyone else or just found her lying there. That would have explained the blood. Lemmy just kept stumm.'

'He would,' said Hal. 'I bet he didn't even give his name.'

'You're right,' grinned Dad.

'That's the Code of the Stittles,' said Hal.

That night, Ellie woke him again. She stood by his

bed, with her duvet wrapped around her and trailing along the floor behind, like a giant caterpillar.

'I couldn't sleep,' she said. 'Can I come in with you?'

'There isn't room.'

'Please, Hal. I won't take up much room. I'll go next to the wall, shall I?' She gathered up her duvet and clambered over him.

Hal was right. There wasn't room. He soon got tired of clinging on to the edge, so he took his duvet and made himself a sort of nest on the floor. After a while, he could tell from Ellie's breathing that she was asleep. He thought of shifting into her bed, but decided to stay where he was, in case she woke up still frightened.

Nine

'Come on, Hal! You'll be late for school.' Mum's voice, reaching him through what seemed like layers of cotton wool.

Hal struggled until his head was free of the duvet. The room was all the wrong way round. His feet were towards the window and his head was by the door.

'Come on, Hal! What are you doing on the floor?'

Hal looked towards the bed. 'Where's Ellie?' he asked

'She looked a bit peaky. I think she might have caught a chill, though goodness knows where at this time of year. Anyway, I told her to go back to bed. But you're all right.'

'But, Mum . . .'

'Come on, or you'll miss the bus.'

'Mum!'

'I must get back to Jack. I've left him in his high chair.'

'It's half-term, Mum!'

'Is it? Oh, sugar! It can't be! Just when I'd got everything worked out.'

But it was.

After she'd gone downstairs again, Hal climbed on to the bed and tried to go back to sleep. But sleeping on the floor had made him stiff. No way could he get comfortable. So he got up and dressed and went downstairs where he found Mum revising her plans for the day.

'I was going to go over to Gran's straight after lunch and clean up a bit. Then get Dad to come home early to look after Jack, so I could take Ellie to see Gran after school. But as there's no school, we could go earlier. Then I could spend the whole afternoon at Gran's tomorrow. But who's going to look after Jack while Ellie and I go to the hospital?'

'I can look after Jack,' said Hal, as she paused for breath. He liked looking after Jack, especially when it was just the two of them on their own.

'Will you? Right. That's settled then.'

Mum was still talking over her shoulder as she

whisked Ellie out of the door. 'I've asked Mrs Next-Door to keep an eye open. Jack should stay in his cot till three at least. You know where to find his potty, don't you? Try to get him to use it if you can. If not, his clean pants are in the top right-hand drawer . . .'

'I know, Mum. You'll miss the bus. See you later.' Hal closed the door behind them and went upstairs.

Jack wasn't asleep. He was standing clutching the bars of his cot, waiting to be fetched downstairs again. Every day about this time they dumped him in his cot. He didn't know why. It was just part of life's rich tapestry.

Hal carried him down and out into the garden. Jack waited to see what would happen next.

'What does the little mouse say, Jack?'

Jack grinned. He knew this game. 'Eeek. Eeek!' he said.

Hal grinned back. 'And what does he do?'

Jack wrinkled his nose. He still hadn't got the hang of wriggling it like Hal did.

'And who's this, Jack?' Hal mimed licking his hand and using it to wash the top of his head and down behind his ears.

'Ho!' yelled Jack. 'Ho!'

'And what does he say?'

Jack let out a miaow so lifelike that next-door's cat leapt up on the fence to see what the excitement was.

After that they did dogs and pigs and monkeys and ducks, tumbling and giggling about on the lawn. But when Hal dropped on to his stomach and wriggled towards him, hissing like a snake, Jack's expression changed to one of alarm and he retreated hastily indoors.

'It's all right, Jack. It's only me. Let's play with the cars now, shall we?'

'Brrm! Brrm!' Jack agreed.

They got out the box of cars and took them down to the rockery at the bottom of the garden. It wasn't a proper rockery, just the rubble left over from making the garden. Every now and then, Mum optimistically pushed bits of plants in, hoping they'd grow, but they never did. A bit of landscaping couldn't do it any harm.

He shifted rocks and smoothed down pathways in the dirt for the cars to run down. The best bits were the cardboard rolls that Ellie had been saving to make some model or other. They made terrific tunnels. The trick was to get the angle of the in-between slope just right, so the cars would run from one tunnel, then change direction as they entered the next. Then if he covered the cardboard over with earth and pebbles . . .

He'd clean forgotten about Jack until he happened to glance up and saw him, with his tummy pressed up against the fence, gazing out across the common. Hal left what he was doing and went over to Jack and crouched down beside him.

'Those are the wild, lonely places, Jack,' he told him, 'where Bisclavret lives. Bisclavret, that's the werewolf. You mustn't be afraid of him, Jack, because there's a bit of him in all of us.' And he began telling Jack the story of Bisclavret, more or less as he'd read it. 'It's not his fault, Jack. He was born that way. The way some people are born with red hair . . .'

Jack sat, solemnly listening. He didn't understand, of course, but he listened, drowsy now, eyelids drooping, sucking on his fingers, and listening. Hal couldn't remember some bits of the story, but he made up for them by putting other bits in. He put in the badgers and made Bisclavret their friend. They never would have been captured, he said, if Bisclavret had been there to defend them. Jack's sleepy eyes gazed past him, out over the common, where Bisclavret roamed.

'I suppose you could say he lived happily ever after, Jack. I suppose you could say that. Just being himself. Happier than a lot of people, anyway.'

He heard a faint sound behind him, like several voices sighing all together. He turned and saw the Stittles clustered just the other side of the fence.

'That was good,' said Rutger. 'That was really good, that was.'

'We were seeing how close we could get without you hearing,' Dustin explained.

'And then, like, we just didn't want to interrupt,' said Harrison.

'Yeah.'

'Yeah.'

'Lemmy's home,' said Michelle.

'That's good,' said Hal.

'Just thought you'd like to know, and – thanks.'

Rutger said, 'We brought you something.' He signalled to the twins, who dived into a clump of bushes and came out carrying armfuls of rhubarb with the leaves still on. 'Sort of a thank-you present,' added Rutger.

Hal tried to remember if he'd ever seen rhubarb growing in the Stittles' garden. It didn't seem very likely. Rhubarb wouldn't stand much chance among the bits of motor bikes and old car tyres and heaps of logs waiting to be sawn up for firewood.

'Er – thanks,' said Hal, offering to take it.

'We'll bring it in, shall we?' said Dustin, stepping over the fence on to the rockery.

'It's no trouble,' said Harrison, following him. After him poured the rest of the Stittles in a steady stream, over the fence, down the rockery and up the garden.

'How's little Nod?' Hal asked Rutger.

'Grandad says to say he's holding his own. How's your gran?'

'OK. A bit dopey from all the pills they keep giving her. I expect she'll rattle when she gets up.'

Rutger grinned. 'I'll send me grandad round when she gets home. He's got a cure for everything.'

Into the kitchen they all trooped and the twins dumped the rhubarb on the table. Hal was wondering how he was going to get them out again, when Michelle, looking past him, said, 'Is he s'posed to do that?'

Jack, toddling after the rest, had paused to admire a butterfly perched on a flower. As he stretched out his hand towards it, the butterfly flew off. Now Jack was picking the flower-heads one by one and tossing them up in the air, either to lure it back or to see if they could fly too.

Hal ran to stop him. 'No, Jack!' he commanded, grabbing hold of his hand.

Jack looked peeved. But he knew how to get his own back. 'Wee-wee?' he said sweetly. He started to shuffle his feet. 'Wee-wee!' he insisted.

'All right, Jack. Wait a minute. Just hang on!' Hal ran back indoors to find the potty, knowing he'd never make it in time.

When he came back, Jack, dressed only in his T-shirt, was peeing among the geraniums, while Michelle stood by, holding his pants and cooing, 'What a good boy he is! What a good boy!'

Madonna was picking up the fallen flower-heads and weaving them into her hair.

'I'd leave 'em off while he's outside,' said Michelle, handing Jack's pants to Hal. 'He won't catch cold. Not this weather.'

The twins had moved back to the rockery and were improving on Hal's excavations. Madonna and Rutger were in the living-room, watching telly. Dolph was standing in front of the bookshelves in the hall.

'Are those all library books?' he said at last.

'Library books?' said Hal. 'No, they're ours. We bought them.'

Dolph stood digesting this novel idea. 'You read 'em all?' he enquired.

'Not those,' said Hal. 'Those are mostly Mum's. Mine are upstairs. Do you want to come and see?'

Dolph nodded and followed him towards the stairs.

'I could lend you one, if you like,' Hal offered. 'If you promise to take care of it. Not that I think you wouldn't,' he added hastily. 'It's just that Mum says I have to be careful who I lend them to.'

He knelt on the bed and started pulling out some of his older books – books he'd finished with. Dolph was only in Ellie's class, after all. Nice bright pictures. Not too much to read.

Dolph pushed them aside. 'Kids' stuff,' he said dismissively. 'What else you got? *Treasure Island.* Read that. *Just William.* He's daft, he is.'

'That was my dad's,' said Hal defensively.

Dolph went on pulling out books and dismissing them as unworthy of attention.

Outside in the garden, Michelle was singing softly to Jack:

'Who's afraid of the big, bad wolf,
Big, bad wolf,
Big, bad wolf?'

Then the doorbell rang. Before Hal could get downstairs, Rutger had it open.

'God bless all here!' came Frank Finnegan's voice. 'Hello there, Hal,' he said, as Hal came down the stairs, with Dolph close on his heels, clutching a copy of *Viking's Dawn*.

Michelle appeared in the kitchen doorway, with a still trouserless Jack in her arms. Behind her the twins jostled one another, trying to see who'd arrived.

'Well, well,' said Frank. 'If I'd known you were having a party, I'd have brought a bottle. Is your dad in, Hal?'

Hal shook his head. 'Sorry. He's not.'

'Ah. I thought he'd arranged to be home early today.'

'He did,' said Hal. 'Then Mum rearranged us all. She's taken Ellie to visit Gran.'

'Ah-ha. How is your granny, by the way?'

'The doctor says there's no real harm done.'

'That's good. All the same, it's a terrible thing to

have happened. What was she doing out there in the middle of the night?'

No one answered.

Rutger looked at Hal. 'We might as well tell him.'

'Can't do any harm now,' Michelle agreed.

'If he was to put it in the paper,' added Dolph, 'it might help to find 'em. Someone might see it and know something and . . .'

'You read too many books,' said Rutger.

'They were after the badgers,' said Hal.

'Badgers?' queried Frank, but before he could get any further the twins cut in.

'And now they've got 'em.'

'She was looking after 'em.'

'And so was Lemmy.'

'Lemmy never done it.'

'He never done nothing.'

'But they said he did and they locked him up.'

'That gave 'em the chance to get in there, see?'

'Whoa!' laughed Frank. 'Let's get things in order.'

'I reckon the police is in it with 'em,' muttered Dolph.

'And I reckon you read too many books,' said Rutger. 'You leave our Lemmy out of it, right?'

'Right,' nodded Frank. 'Do you mind if I take a

few notes? I think we might have a story here. Now let's start from the beginning. Where exactly are these badgers?'

'We don't know,' said Harrison.

'That's the whole point,' said Dustin. 'Somebody's got 'em.'

'Shut up,' said Rutger. 'I'll do the talkin'. There were these badgers, right, livin' in that bit of wood on the edge of the common . . .'

'Mindin' their own business,' put in Dolph.

Rutger glared at him. 'You tell him, Hal,' he said. 'I'll keep this lot from interrupting.'

Nobody else said anything after that, while Hal told the tale of the badgers again.

'Do you think you could show me the place?' asked Frank when he'd finished. 'Maybe we could take some pictures. I've got a camera with me. Then perhaps Mr Cornish could come round and take a picture of the little girl and the badger cub.'

From the living-room, above the sound of the telly, came Madonna's voice: 'I'm not a little girl!'

The rest of the Stittles looked at one another, holding a silent conference.

'All right,' Rutger agreed. 'We'll show you. You coming, Hal? Michelle can look after the littl'un.'

Hal checked the time. 'I can't,' he said. 'Mum'll be back soon.'

Regretfully he watched as the Stittles left the way they had come, up the rockery and over the fence, taking Frank Finnegan with them.

'I'll phone your dad tonight,' said Frank. 'OK? Or if not, tell him I'll meet him at Polly Froggett's as arranged.'

Dolph went last, clutching *Viking's Dawn* to his chest. 'Next time,' he said, 'we'll bring you some carrots.'

'There's no need,' said Hal. 'Really there's not.'

'It's no trouble,' said Dolph. 'There's a whole field of 'em just opposite ours.'

The house seemed empty without the Stittles, though there were traces of them everywhere. Hal put Jack's pants back on, popped him back in his cot and set about tidying up. There was nothing he could do about the rhubarb. Even if he'd crammed it into the dustbin, Mum would be bound to see it next time she opened the lid.

The first thing she said when she walked into the kitchen was, 'Where did all this rhubarb come from?'

'Oh, um, somebody brought it,' Hal said vaguely.

'Didn't they say who?'

He shrugged. 'They asked how Gran was.'

'She was funny,' said Ellie.

'That's good,' said Hal. 'If she's making jokes.'

'I didn't mean funny ha-ha, fat-head! I meant funny weird. You remember that film where everybody looked the same but they weren't really the same, because they were aliens made to look like them, growing in pods . . .'

'Don't be silly, Ellie,' said Mum. 'She was just a bit quiet, that's all. It's the tablets. I think it's doing her a lot of good – plenty of rest, and proper care and a regular routine.'

'That's what I mean,' said Ellie. 'Yes, nurse. No, nurse. Three bags full, nurse. She's not like our gran at all.'

Ten

At lunchtime next day, Mum threw a wobbly.

'I'm sorry,' said Dad. 'But I can't take the kids with me this afternoon.'

'You've done it before,' she said, rattling the dishes in the sink so fiercely that one of them broke clean across.

'Fêtes and flower shows,' said Dad. 'Not private houses. We can't all troop up to Polly Froggett's as if we've been invited to tea.'

Mum stood poised, with the pieces of the broken plate one in each hand, as if she might be able to fit them together again, if she could only remember how. Dad took them from her and shoved them in the bin. 'Why can't they come with you?' he asked her.

'I've got to get the cottage straight. I was going to

do it yesterday and then ...' She wiped a hand across her forehead, leaving a trail of bubbles. 'I just don't want them under my feet.'

'Leave them here. They'll be all right.'

'Will they?'

Hal had seen Mrs Next-Door that morning, 'having a word' with Mum over the fence about the Stittle invasion.

In the end, Dad bundled Hal and Ellie into the car, drove them down to Polly Froggett's and left them in it, parked outside the massive iron gates. Hal had snatched up a book to read on the way out, but Ellie couldn't even switch on the radio, because Dad had taken the keys. She sat fiddling with the steering-wheel, half-heartedly muttering, 'Brrm, brrm.'

'Don't do that,' said Hal, without looking up. 'Dad says it ruins the tyres.'

'I know,' she snapped.

'And don't touch the gear lever, in case the brake's not on.'

'I *know*. I'm not *stupid*.' She wound down the window and wound it up again. 'She's up to something,' she said.

'Who?'

'Mum.'

'What do you mean?'

'Why didn't she want us to go with her? We could have *helped*.'

Hal grunted non-committally and tried to concentrate on his book. Ellie pushed the lighter in and fiddled with the wing-mirrors while she waited for it to pop out again. She was searching the glove compartment for stray sweets when a rapping on the window made them both jump.

Miss Letty Harding was peering in at them. 'What are you doing here?' she asked.

Ellie wound down the window. 'I'm Eleanor May Cornish,' she said. 'And this is my brother Hal.'

'I know *who* you are,' replied Miss Letty patiently. 'You're Mrs Cornish's grandchildren. I asked you what you are doing outside my niece's house.'

'Dad's inside,' explained Hal, 'taking pictures for the *Mercury*.'

'And he left you out here? It's much too hot to sit in a car. Come along. Out you get.'

Obediently they both got out of the car. Miss Letty pressed the intercom by the gate.

'Who is it?' A breathless little voice.

'It's me, dear.'

'Oh, hello, Aunty.'

'I thought I'd drop in, just to see how things are going.'

'Things?'

'With the gentlemen of the Press?'

'Oh, yes! Just a minute.'

The gates swung open. Hal checked that the car doors were locked and followed Ellie through the iron gate after Miss Letty, who strode on without checking to see if they were following. He heard the gates clang shut behind them. Alcatraz. Somewhere behind the steel-shuttered windows, the vast kitchen extension, the Chinese garden room and the fake Tudor chimneys a pretty little Georgian vicarage was serving a life sentence for a crime it hadn't committed.

Hal couldn't imagine why Dad and Frank were bothering with Polly Froggett's. There were dozens of nicer houses about with more interesting people living in them. Dad was going to have a hard time making it look even half as good as the Manor House, where Miss Letty lived. The Manor House was real Tudor from the chimneys down, built of red bricks made from local clay, with high, timbered gables.

'All I had to do was point the camera,' Dad had said modestly, as he laid the photos out on the table. 'Every one's a winner!'

Inside the house, the pictures showed room after room with warm, dark panelling, carved beams and whitewashed walls. Sunlight shone through mullioned windows making rainbow patterns on the floor. Through five hundred years of history Miss Letty walked or sat with easy confidence. At the bottom of the stairs she paused, with her head a little on one side, as if listening politely to the ghost of some long-dead ancestor.

They walked up the gravel drive in silence. Miss Letty didn't seem to go in for chat, but she was a very reassuring person to have around. Mrs Harding-Froggett certainly seemed to think so, judging from the relief on her face as she flung open the front door.

'Come in, Aunty! I could do with a bit of moral support. I was so afraid you weren't coming after all! I know you said you might, but . . .'

'I'm not late, am I?' enquired Miss Letty, offering her cheek to be kissed.

'Of course not, Aunty! You're never late. But Dan and Mr Finnegan got here a bit early and I've been holding the fort sort of but I can't think of a thing to say, well, nothing worth putting in the paper.'

'I shouldn't worry,' said Miss Letty calmly. 'I'm sure Mr Finnegan will be quite happy to invent something. He probably prefers it. Do you know Miss Eleanor May Cornish and her brother Hal?'

'No. Well, yes, but not since Ellie was in her pram. How big you've grown! Oops, sorry, I suppose I shouldn't have said that . . .'

She seemed about to shake hands, changed her mind and gave them a nervous little smile instead. She stood with her hands hanging limply level with her waist. Like a little squirrel, thought Hal. Ready to bolt at any moment. A squirrel in a frilly dress. Hair fluffed up, like a squirrel's tail.

'Well, well!' she said. 'What are we going to do with you?'

'Feed them,' advised Frank Finnegan, appearing in a doorway halfway along the passage, with a wine glass in his hand. 'Feed them and water them and put them out to grass.'

'Drinking, Mr Finnegan?' exclaimed Miss Letty. 'At this time of day?'

Frank grinned at her. 'Will you join us?'

'I think I'll make myself a cup of tea.'

Dad was in the kitchen, drinking bottled beer.

'I expect you two would like Coke to drink,' said Mrs Harding-Froggett. 'I think we've got some. I'll go and look.' She scurried off.

Ellie said she'd prefer tea, please. Ellie only drank tea when she was out, never at home. Hal said he'd have the Coke. One day, if he drank enough of it, he might actually get to like the stuff. He sat turning the glass round and round, wondering vaguely why the ice always stayed in the same place.

'Why don't you go and amuse yourselves in the garden?' Dad suggested. 'Is that all right, Jenny?'

'Of course,' beamed Mrs Harding-Froggett.

'And we'll let the men look round by themselves, so they can choose the best locations – is that the word? – while we find something suitable for you to wear for the photographs,' said Miss Letty.

Mrs Harding-Froggett plucked at the frilly dress. 'Oh, but Garth thought . . .'

'I daresay he did,' remarked Miss Letty, leading her away.

Hal and Ellie found themselves outside on the patio. 'Amuse yourselves in the garden' is easily said. It's not always easy to do. There was a swimming pool, of course, but they hadn't brought their swimming things. There was a tennis court, but no sign of rackets and balls. The lawn was the sort that usually has a big sign saying *Keep off the Grass*.

Round the back, between the house and the stables, they came upon the pens where the dogs were kept. It looked as if one of them had been trying to tunnel its way out, but now all three were snoozing in the shade, until they heard the first crunch of footsteps on gravel. Suddenly they were up and raising the alarm, one, two, three, barking in three-part harmony. A voice shouted from the direction of the stables. A door opened and Hal caught a glimpse of the figure of a man, before a flying weight caught him in the ribs and knocked him sprawling. He landed half-in and half-out of a bed of evergreens, with Ellie on top of him.

'What did you do that for?' he demanded, as soon as he got his breath back.

'Keep down!' hissed Ellie. 'It's Rambo.'

'The man in the stables? So what? We've got permission to be here.'

'Yes, but what's *he* doing here?' Ellie, still on hands and knees, peered cautiously round the bushes.

The dogs, who had been on the point of settling

down, saw Ellie and at once set up a frantic barking again. Rambo swore at them. He looked around, but saw nothing odd. It must be frustrating, being a dog. Like the audience at the pantomime, yelling, 'Behind you! Look behind you!' Rambo, like Widow Twankey, looking round. What's the matter? There's nothing there. Behind you! In the end the dogs gave up in disgust.

Rambo turned away, moving back towards the stables. That was when Hal noticed another figure, in the shadows by the house wall. He must have been standing perfectly still while the dogs were barking, but now he moved again. Frank Finnegan.

Of course, he had a right to be there, just as much as Hal and Ellie. He'd taken Miss Letty at her word and was looking round. But there was something about the way he moved which stopped them calling out to him. Something shifty in the way he glanced about, keeping all the while to the narrow strip of grass between the gravel path and the flowerbed by the house wall.

Hal's gaze flipped towards Rambo, ambling back the way he'd come. Would he get back inside before Frank reached the corner? Would the dogs bark and give the alarm? Would it matter?

Frank reached the corner of the house and, after another glance round, jumped clear across the gravel path and set off across the grass towards the stables. He was being so careful to watch his back, he didn't seem to have noticed Rambo straight ahead. The dogs made no sound, but suddenly Rambo stopped. He turned around.

He saw Frank Finnegan at the exact moment Frank caught sight of him. They both looked startled. Then Frank smiled. And Rambo smiled back and called out something. They walked towards each other and started chatting away like old friends.

Hal and Ellie crawled back behind the bushes and sat looking at one another.

'He knows him,' said Hal.

'He's one of Them.'

'Hold on, Ellie. We don't even know that they are Them. It might not be what it looks like. Frank must know loads of people.' Why am I making excuses for him? wondered Hal. I never liked him; whereas Ellie . . .

The conversation over, Frank Finnegan went back the way he had come, walking on the path once he reached the house, with a jaunty look about him. Hal and Ellie moved round the little clump of bushes,

154

keeping out of his line of sight.

They sat in silence for a moment. Then Ellie said, 'I'm going to take a look in there. Come on!'

'Do I have to?' Hal groaned.

But Ellie was away, across the grass, bent double, looking about as sinister as it's possible to look without wearing a mask and carrying a bag marked SWAG. Hal sighed and went after her. They reached the end wall of the stables without being seen.

'Now, hoist me up,' said Ellie.

Hal leaned back against the wall and made a stirrup with his hands. Ellie put her foot in it and he lifted her until she could see in at the window.

'What can you see?'

'Nothing much. It's just a room. There seem to be a lot of little rooms, all leading into one another. The bit for the horses must be up the other end.'

'Polly Froggett hasn't got any horses.'

'You know what I mean. What does he keep in here, anyway? I can hear noises . . . And there's a smell of . . . Oh, sugar! I think he's coming back. Let me down. Let me down!'

'Ouch! That's my foot.'

'Sorry.'

'Did he see you?'

155

'I'm not sure. I don't think so.'

'Boo!' said a voice behind them. They spun round. 'Caught you,' said Miss Letty cheerfully. 'Who was the quarry?' She was tall enough to peer in the window without a bunk-up.

At that moment Rambo appeared round the corner of the building. 'Oh, it's you, Skinner,' she said. 'Did we frighten you?' Rambo scowled and grunted. 'Well, we won't keep you from your work. Come along, children.'

As she strode off briskly across the lawn, the dogs began barking again. 'Sit! Down!' commanded Miss Letty, without pausing in her stride. As one dog, they sat.

'We used to play that game,' she said, 'when I was young. Pick out a quarry and follow them all round the village without being seen. Harry Stittle – old Mr Stittle, as he now is – he was the one! He had a way of standing stock-still, so he seemed to blend into the scenery, almost invisible. Quite extra-ordinary.'

'Who was that man?' asked Ellie.

'Mr Skinner? He does odd jobs for my niece's husband now and then. Horrid little man. Next time you play, I should find a quarry who isn't so likely to mind if he catches you. The postman, say. Or the milkman.'

When they got back to the house, they found Mrs Harding-Froggett alone on the patio. She looked less like a squirrel now, in a plain cotton dress, with a white blazer and her hair brushed so that it moved about.

'Where's Frank?' asked Ellie.

'He's gone,' she said. 'Your father's in the kitchen.'

'Come along, Eleanor,' said Miss Letty. 'You can help me clear away the tea things.'

Ellie went, without a word. Hal was left with Mrs Harding-Froggett, both trying to think of something to say.

Then Polly Froggett arrived home, in time to have his picture taken for the papers. Dressed in hired hunting pink, Mr Harding-Froggett posed nervously beside a large chestnut horse borrowed specially for the afternoon from a friend in the racing business.

Eleven

By the time they got home, Mum had been back long enough to do a load of washing. She was pegging out Gran's net curtains on the line to dry.

'Can somebody have a look and see what Jack's doing?' She called out. 'He's been a little pest all afternoon. Wouldn't even eat his banana.'

Dad was already making for his workroom in the garage. Ellie walked straight through to the living-room to switch on the telly. Hal found Jack sitting on the kitchen floor, eating Rice Krispies out of the packet. Each time he took a fistful, he scattered dozens more on the floor around him.

'They taste better with milk on,' Hal told him. 'Want to try some?'

Jack let himself be lifted into his high chair. With

two fingers stuck in his mouth and the other hand twiddling his ear, he watched Hal measuring out the cereal, pouring the milk. 'Want some sugar, Jack?'

No answer. That was probably a yes.

'Of course,' he said, 'what it really needs now is a sliced-up banana on top.'

Jack glared at him, seized the spoon he offered and began tucking in. Hal fetched a dustpan and brush and started clearing up the mess on the floor.

'Hal!' Ellie's voice came from the living-room. 'Hal, come and look at this!'

'Just a minute,' called Hal, busily sweeping under the table.

'I said, come and look!'

Hal left what he was doing and let himself be dragged into the living-room.

'Look!'

He looked. He saw a lot of things that weren't usually there. Gran's china shepherdess that Aunt May had brought back from Germany. The marquetry music box from Prague. The two brass candlesticks that Gran kept handy in case of power cuts. The pretty little vase with the letter M picked out in forget-me-nots, the first present Grandad ever bought her. Most surprisingly of all, Gran's marble clock with the gilt cherubs was ticking merrily away on the mantelpiece.

'I told you she was up to something,' said Ellie triumphantly.

They met Mum as she was coming back into the kitchen with the empty washing basket.

'What's Gran's clock doing in our living-room?' demanded Ellie.

'Well, it's actually working for a start,' said Mum cheerfully. 'There was nothing wrong with it. It just needed winding. I found the key tucked down the back. Gran must have forgotten where she put it.'

'She didn't forget,' said Ellie. 'That clock was stopped on purpose.'

'Oh, Ellie! Whatever for?'

'I don't know. I just know there was a reason.'

'Oh, well, we can always stop it again, if that's what she wants.'

'What's it doing here, anyway?' asked Ellie. 'And all the other things?'

'I thought they'd be safer here. With the cottage empty and standing all on its own, anyone could break in and help themselves. I had the feeling somebody's been in there already. The kitchen floor was filthy.'

'That'll be me,' said Dad, coming in from the garage. 'Sorry.'

Mum ignored him. 'It wouldn't surprise me,' she went on, 'if Lemmy Stittle's been nosing around. I saw him in the garden when I got there. He soon took himself off when he saw me. Anyway, there's nothing missing, as far as I could tell. Though there's so much junk . . . Newspapers dating back donkey's years. Boxes full of jamjars. I've put a lot out by the dustbin, Dan, for you to take down to the bottle bank. Oh! There was one thing. One of the drawers is missing from that pretty little tallboy in the spare bedroom.'

Dad glanced at Hal and Ellie. 'I'll have a look for it next time I go round,' he promised.

Hal busied himself getting Jack out of his high chair.

Ellie asked, 'What's for tea?'

'I haven't thought,' said Mum.

'Fish and chips?' suggested Ellie. 'Hal and I can go.'

'Good idea,' said Dad, taking out his wallet.

'Come on,' said Ellie.

'It's too soon,' protested Hal. 'The van won't be there for ages yet.'

'We can wait. Come on.'

As he fetched his bike out, Hal heard a crash from the kitchen and remembered the dustpan full of Rice Krispies that he'd left on the floor. Too late. He cycled down the road after Ellie.

The mobile fish-and-chip shop toured the surrounding villages, taking a different route each night, but always beginning and ending at the corner by the new estate. Ellie didn't stop at the corner. She turned sharp right and cycled on.

'Ellie! Where are you going, Ellie?'

Ellie only cycled faster, half-standing up on the pedals, the bike swaying dangerously.

'Ellie!'

He winced as she stuck out an arm and turned right again, with no more than a quick glance over her shoulder to check for cars. He was more careful. He knew where she was heading for now. Gran's house, of course.

By the time he got there, Ellie's bike was lying on the front path with one wheel still spinning, while Ellie, balanced on an upturned bucket, was trying to see in the kitchen window. Hal leaned his bike up against the hedge and joined her.

Mum had tried to make up for taking the net

curtains down by drawing the others part way across but, by pressing his forehead up against the glass, he could still make out most of Gran's kitchen, looking unnaturally tidy. Not a dirty cup on the draining-board. Not a newspaper. The cushions on the couch plumped up, the shawl neatly folded.

'Where's my sheep's skull?' frowned Ellie.

The mantelpiece was bare.

'Where's Cyril the squirrel?' Hal wondered.

'That skull was mine,' said Ellie. 'I only lent it to Gran to look after 'cause Mum was going to throw it away.'

She jumped down from the bucket and set off round the back of the house. But the window of the downstairs loo was tight shut.

Just as well, thought Hal. Ellie was a good bit wider than Madonna. She'd never have made it without getting stuck.

Muttering crossly to herself, Ellie led the way back round the front, to the dustbin. She climbed on to one of the bales of old newspapers stacked beside it and flung back the lid.

'Look at that!' she said.

The dustbin was crammed full. On top was the old Oxo tin in which Gran saved odd bits of string.

Underneath, neatly clipped together, were piles of paper bags sorted into different sizes. Gran had never lost the wartime habit of saving every little thing that one day might possibly come in useful. Old teacups with no handles. Tins of food with the price in old money. Spare bits of carpet and odd balls of wool.

'She's got no right,' said Ellie, delving deeper. 'She's got no right to throw Gran's stuff away without asking.'

'Perhaps she did ask her,' said Hal reasonably. 'Perhaps she asked her in the hospital.'

He left her still rummaging and wandered off down the garden. Mum said she'd sent Lemmy away. But now he was back, quietly hoeing between the rows of vegetables. He wouldn't desert Gran's garden while there was work to do. Above him on the red-brick wall, Uncle Ho lay soaking up the sun.

Hal spotted an early strawberry nestling among the leaves. He picked it, dusted it off and popped it in his mouth. Magic! The taste of summer sunshine.

Lemmy looked up and smiled.

Hal smiled back. 'How's little Nod?' he asked.

'He's mending. Lonely, though.'

'Is there any trace of the rest of them?'

Lemmy shook his head. He hoed in silence for a while, then, 'I never should have let it happen,' he said. 'I should have been there.'

'You couldn't help it, Lemmy. The police locked you up.'

Lemmy turned his head away, a picture of utter dejection, like a dog that's been punished unfairly. Then he turned back to Hal and smiled. 'I said nothing!' he said proudly.

It was no good pointing out that if he had said something, they might have let him go a bit sooner. 'Did you see what happened, Lemmy? Did Gran really just fall?'

Lemmy's lips set in a firm line: he wasn't going to be punished again. 'Rutger says to say nothing.'

'I'm not the police, Lemmy. You can talk to me.'

Lemmy rested his hoe against the wall. He went over to the garden shed and came back with a basket. He began picking peas in the same unhurried way that he did everything, his big hands gently checking each pod to see if it was ready, before nipping it off and dropping it into the basket.

'I tried to look after 'er,' he said softly. 'Wipe the blood off. Keep 'er warm.'

'You didn't think of going for help?'

'Couldn't.'

'You could have sent Ellie. You must have seen Ellie.'

'She were frightened. Didn't want to frighten 'er more.'

'Ellie's never been frightened of you.'

' 'S different at night.' A grin spread over his face. 'I frightened them off, though! Frightened them, good and proper.' He shook his head. 'Didn't want to frighten her.'

Hal was puzzled, but before he could ask any more questions, Lemmy thrust the basket at him. 'You take 'em.'

Hal automatically took the basket. Then slowly he gave it back. 'I can't,' he explained. 'We're not supposed to be here. We're supposed to be buying fish and chips. Oh, sugar! Ellie!'

An answering shout came from the direction of the dustbin.

'We've got to go,' said Hal apologetically.

'I'll leave 'em in the porch, then, shall I?'

'The peas? Sure. Good idea. Dad will find them in the morning.'

Ellie, flushed with triumph, stood waiting by the

bikes. 'Where did you go?' she asked. 'I found it. My skull. And Cyril the squirrel. And Gran's pictures.' She was packing them all into her bike basket. 'Imagine throwing those away! I don't care if she did have permission.'

'Hurry up,' Hal pleaded. 'Or we'll miss the van altogether. Then what are we going to tell Mum?'

They arrived back at the bottom of their road just as the van was pulling away. It was a funny thing: every time Hal tried to ride no-handed, he fell off, but if, like now, he did it without thinking, it was easy. He raced head-on towards the fish-and-chip van, his arms going like windmills until the driver pulled into the kerb again.

Hal had to take the fish and chips, because Ellie was carrying all the bits and pieces she'd salvaged from Gran's dustbin. She flounced upstairs with them as soon as they got home and didn't say a word to Mum all evening.

Next morning, Hal picked out *The Road to Miklagard* from his bookshelf.

'I'm just going round to –' he lowered his voice – 'Dolph Stittle's,' he told Mum as he went through the kitchen.

'Who?' she called after him.

'Just a friend.'

He escaped before she could ask again, first at a run, then slowing to a walk, making for the far end of the village and the brick council house where the Stittles lived – all of them, except old Mr Stittle. He still lived in the old gamekeeper's cottage, with no electricity, one cold-water tap and a loo at the bottom of the garden. He preferred it. How the rest all fitted into the council house was a mystery, unless it was a lot bigger inside than out.

Hal knocked at the door. There was plenty of noise from inside, but no one came to answer it.

'Hello!' called Hal.

A face appeared at an upstairs window. Dolph. His face creased into a smile when he saw Hal. 'Hello,' he said. 'What you doin' down here?'

'Enjoying the book?' enquired Hal.

'It's mega!'

'I thought, when you've finished that, you might like to read the next one.' Hal took *The Road to Miklagard* out of his pocket and brandished it.

'Cheers,' said Dolph. 'I'll come down.' There was a thundering of feet on the stairs. Then Dolph appeared at the front door.

'Actually,' said Hal, 'I wanted to have a word with you all. About Lemmy.'

'What about him?' Suddenly Dolph was on the defensive.

'From what Lemmy said . . .'

'What did he say?'

'Not much. You've all drummed the rule, *say nothing*, so firmly into his head . . .'

'Good.'

'You ought to let him tell the police what he knows.'

'No way!'

'I think he saw what happened to Gran.'

'So?'

'He knows who those men are. If they're not the ones who took the badgers, they probably know who did.'

'Good thinking,' said Dolph.

'Well?'

'Don't worry.' Dolph patted him kindly on the shoulder. 'It's all being taken care of. We'll keep you posted.' He flourished *The Road to Miklagard* as he turned towards the house. 'Thanks for the book.'

'Oh, by the way,' said Hal. 'Mum's noticed that drawer is missing . . .'

'No problem!'

Next morning when Hal fetched in the milk, he found a bunch of carrots on the step, packed into the missing drawer. He hid it in the garden shed, before he took the carrots indoors.

'Where did those come from?' Mum wondered.

Hal shrugged. 'Probably the same place as the rhubarb.'

Twelve

The rest of the week was all comings and goings and toings and froings. They ate odd meals at odd times, Ellie ran out of clean socks, and Hal had to run down to the village shop on early closing day and knock on the back door because they'd run out of loo rolls.

It reminded him of the time when Jack was born, at two minutes after midnight on Christmas morning, a full two weeks early – just so he could get his picture in the paper, according to Ellie. She was miffed because in the excitement no one had remembered to fill up the stocking at the end of her bed. It was no good Aunt May wittering on about 'the lovely baby brother Father Christmas has brought you'. Ellie wanted proper presents, at the proper time. And a proper Christmas dinner. They had to have sausages, because no one had got round to defrosting the turkey. When Hal and Ellie were finally packed off to Gran's for the rest of the holiday, it was like two desert travellers sighting an oasis.

This week was a bit like that. But now it was Gran, not Mum, who was in hospital, so there was no refuge there. Every day either Mum or Dad popped in to see how she was. Most of the rest of Mum's time was spent over at the cottage. One evening she took the car and brought back several of the nicest bits of furniture. They stood about the house looking awkward and out of place, like party guests who'd arrived too early. Mrs Next-Door kept popping in with offerings of food for the children – 'to save you having to cook' – or to take to Gran. Hard on her heels came the cat, arching his back whenever he caught sight of Uncle Ho, and making threatening noises before taking cover behind his mistress's fat legs.

Each time this happened, Uncle Ho just sat, staring him out. Sometimes he yawned. The intruder got braver. He ventured closer. Each time Hal watched with interest, as Uncle Ho sat, biding his time. The cat came closer still. He swished his tail and flattened back his ears and he snarled. Uncle Ho stood up and slowly stretched himself.

While next-door's cat was still wondering what his next move ought to be, something like a guided missile struck him head-on and the world exploded in a mass of flying fur. He gave a howl and headed for sanctuary, overshot and sent Mrs Next-Door crashing to the kitchen floor. On he plunged, with Uncle Ho close behind, into the living-room, where he tried to escape up the chimney, but only succeeded in bringing down a load of soot.

Three times round the room they went, leaving three sooty trails, before the cat remembered what doors were for and shot upstairs to wake Jack from his afternoon nap. After him streaked Uncle Ho, stopping sensibly short of the window, while his quarry launched himself into space. Luckily he landed on the roof of the utility room. From there, he limped towards home.

Mum arrived back from another afternoon cleaning the cottage to find soot all round the living-room, claw marks the length of the hall, Jack bawling upstairs and Mrs Next-Door sitting on the kitchen floor in a pool of cold soup. Uncle Ho sprawled on the doorstep, quietly washing himself.

'That cat!' Mrs Next-Door pointed an accusing finger.

'Uncle Ho?' said Ellie, picking him up. 'He's a lovely cat! Aren't you? Aren't you a lovely cat?'

And Uncle Ho, who *never* let himself be cuddled, smirked and purred agreement.

So the next day (which was Saturday), Mum locked up the house in the afternoon and took Jack with her, while Dad drove Hal and Ellie to the hospital to visit Gran.

In the car park, in one of the spaces marked *Doctors Only*, Hal spotted a red Mini familiar to everyone in Laxworth. Old Mr Stittle stood beside it, while Mrs Stittle got herself comfy in the driving seat. The words 'quart' and 'pint pot' sprang to mind. Though no car could have done justice to Beryl, Mother of the Stittle Tribe. A chariot would have been more like it: a chariot, with four horses galloping abreast, and knives on the wheels, and her straw-coloured hair streaming in the wind.

As soon as she saw Dad, she heaved herself out again, grabbed him by both shoulders and planted a kiss on his cheek. 'Danny, boy! How you doing? We've just been to see your mum. Haven't we, Dad?'

'Hello, Beryl.' Dad checked his cheek for lipstick as he shook hands with Mr Stittle. 'Harry.'

Mr Stittle gravely shook hands with Dad, then took Hal by surprise by shaking hands with him too. He had the most amazing eyes, very bright, one green, one blue. Hal was fascinated by them. The old man hung on to his hand for what seemed a very long time, then nodded to himself, as if satisfied, before he let go.

Ellie got only a glance and 'Good-day, little lady.'

'What do you think, Harry?' Dad asked, as if old Mr Stittle really was some sort of doctor.

The old man shook his head. 'She ain't herself, and that's a fact.'

'And she won't be, till she's back in her own place again,' put in Mrs Stittle.

'Hospitals!' The old man glared up at the building.

'We took her a few bits and pieces,' said Mrs Stittle.

'That was kind of you,' said Dad.

'Did you know,' said Mr Stittle, 'that forty-two per cent of patients catch something while they're actually in the hospital?'

'Is that so?'

'It was in the *Reader's Digest*.'

'Well, what do you expect, Dad,' said Mrs Stittle, squeezing herself into the driving seat again. 'All those sick people, locked up together.'

'You get her home,' advised Mr Stittle. 'Or I won't answer for the consequences.' He climbed into the little red car and they chugged away, hugging the white line in the middle of the road.

Upstairs, Dad's first job was to help the nurse push Gran's bed back into place. It seemed the Stittles had it fixed in their minds that an invalid always got better quicker if the bed was lined up north to south.

From the bedside cabinet, the nurse picked up the first of their offerings, a six-pack of Guinness, and handed it to Dad. 'I think you'd better find a home for that,' she said. 'The jar of honey can stay. What on earth's this?' Between her finger and thumb she held a bag of dead leaves. She sniffed it. 'I hope there's nothing alive in there.'

'I think,' said Dad, 'it's probably some kind of herbal tea.' Into the pedal-bin it went, without more ado.

Which left the basket of eggs. The nurse picked it up. 'We'll be discharging you in a day or two, Mrs

Cornish,' she said. 'You can take these with you to The Lawns.'

'Gran doesn't live at The Lawns,' said Hal. The Lawns was one of Polly Froggett's old people's homes.

'She will soon,' said the nurse brightly. 'Won't that be nice?'

'It'd be horrible,' said Ellie. 'The Lawns is full of old people.'

'Senior citizens, dear,' the nurse corrected her. 'It's not very nice to call them old.'

But she is old, Hal thought miserably, looking at the frail figure in the bed. It was like Mr Stittle said, she wasn't herself. There was something missing: as if her self was wandering far away and without it she was slowly turning into the meek little old lady she'd pretended to be for Mum's benefit.

'You're not moving to The Lawns, are you, Gran?' demanded Ellie.

Gran looked uncertainly from Ellie to the nurse and then to Dad. 'I haven't quite made up my mind,' she said at last. And you could tell she was just waiting for someone to make it up for her. 'I think Barbara may be right,' she said to Dad.

Ellie flashed a triumphant look at Hal. The look

said, didn't I tell you she was up to something?

'If I was to sell the cottage to Polly Froggett,' Gran went on, 'oh, I know the offer's not as good as the one he made before, but house prices have gone down and now he's had a chance to look round, he says there's a lot that wants doing to it ... but it would still be enough to pay for my keep.'

'I'm sure your daughter-in-law only wants what's best for you, Mrs Cornish,' came from the nurse.

'I'm sure she does,' Gran agreed. 'And I've been very selfish and given you all such a lot of trouble. You must have been worried sick this past week, and you'll go on worrying as long as I go on living alone. Oh dear, I suddenly feel all weepy. Pass me those tissues, will you?'

'It's just the tablets,' said Dad.

Gran blew her nose. 'So many tablets! Goodness knows what they're all for. They never tell you properly.'

Dad said, 'You must do what you want, Mum. If you decide to stay in the cottage, I can come round every day, to check that you're all right. Twice a day, if you like.'

Gran shook her head. 'I don't want that.'

'I could come round after school,' offered Hal.

'That was what Mum kept saying before we moved,' said Ellie. 'She kept on and on, saying we ought to be nearer Gran, in case anything happened, and now it has.'

'I don't want to give you all that trouble,' said Gran.

'You'll be no trouble to anyone at The Lawns,' said the nurse. 'There are people there paid to keep an eye on you night and day.'

No more wandering in the moonlight then, thought Hal. No watching badgers by owl–light. Regular mealtimes and day-time TV and bingo once a week, as a treat.

'They wait on you hand and foot. You'll never need to make another cup of tea, or wash a plate.'

Or make your own bread, or spin a fleece, pick peas and eat them straight from the pod, or splash in puddles and scuff through the autumn leaves . . .

'You're lucky they were able to find you a place at such short notice. I envy you, I really do!'

'Then why don't *you* move there?' snapped Ellie. 'You're not moving to The Lawns, are you, Gran?'

Gran didn't answer. She just sat plucking nervously at the bed-covers.

'You'll see, it's all for the best,' chirruped the nurse.

Ellie flashed her a look of pure hatred.

Hal said nothing. He just wanted to go home.

As they were going down the stairs on their way out, he said to Dad, 'Is Gran like that because she hit her head?'

Dad put an arm round his shoulders. 'Not in the way you mean. The doctor says there's no physical damage. But it shakes you up, a thing like that. Destroys your confidence.'

'You knew, didn't you?' said Ellie. 'About packing Gran off to The Lawns.'

'We'd talked about it, yes,' he admitted. 'Nothing's been decided yet. But it just so happens there's a room free. There might not be another one for some time. So Gran's got to make up her mind quickly.'

'And you weren't going to tell us. You weren't even going to ask us what we thought!'

What difference would it have made, if they had? thought Hal. What kids thought didn't come into it. In the end, the grown-ups always went ahead and did what they wanted anyway. You just had to make the best of it.

'Don't get on at Mum when we get home, Ellie,'

Dad pleaded. 'You'll only make things worse.'

'I won't say a word to her,' said Ellie.

If Mum knew she'd been sent to Coventry, she gave no sign of it. She sang quietly to herself as she ironed Gran's bedroom curtains and seemed so unconcerned about whether Jack ate his tea or not that he polished off a boiled egg and soldiers without a murmur of protest.

Upstairs in Ellie's room, Hal perched on the edge of the bed and stared at the two photos of Gran propped up on the dressing-table. There was the real Gran, if she was anywhere. Muffled up in winter woollies with her *Ban the Bomb* banner. Draped in cheesecloth, offering a flower to one of the policemen arresting her outside the American Embassy. Her hair was brown then, instead of grey. But those pictures were more like the Gran of a week ago than that frail little figure in the hospital bed. He kept telling himself that a lot of old people would jump at the chance to live in a place where they'd be warm and well fed, with plenty of company.

Ellie came in. 'Don't touch those,' she said. 'They're mine.'

'They're Gran's,' Hal corrected her quietly.

'Yes.' Ellie sat down beside him on the bed.

She looks a lot like Gran, thought Hal. Same eyes. Same way of holding her head. Ready to take on the world.

'It was all a plot from the beginning,' said Ellie, 'so Polly Froggett could steal Gran's house. I bet he paid those men to beat up Gran, so she'd be out of the way. He knew Mum'd be easy to deal with.'

'Dad says . . .'

'Dad's useless. He'll go along with whatever Mum decides. Mum gets Gran's furniture.'

'Ellie!'

'Well, Gran won't have room for it, will she? Not if she moves to The Lawns!'

'You're talking rubbish, Ellie, and you know it. Those men weren't after Gran. It was the badgers they were after. Gran just happened to be in the wrong place at the wrong time.'

'You know something?' said Ellie miserably.

'What?'

'She never mentioned the badgers once. I was dreading having to tell her and she never even asked.'

In his own room, Hal pulled a chair up to the

window and sat curled up, watching the shadows darkening in corners until they felt strong enough to send out thin fingers to steal a little of the daylight. Then a little more. And more. Until only the treetops were left standing out against the evening sky. Bats wheeled and soared in the dusk. The moon came out. The evening star, and more stars, in ones and twos, then whole clusters of them. Half in a dream he watched them. Again he had the odd feeling that the everyday world was dissolving away and only the wilderness was real. Unchanging. This time he found it comforting.

Bisclavret.

Had he said it aloud, or only thought it? There, on the edge of the common, a shape seemed to be forming itself out of the shadows. A creature very like a dog, but thinner, its grey fur gleaming in the moonlight. It lifted its head, looking up at the house with sad, wise eyes. Bisclavret?

Bisclavret, help me. I don't know what to do.

From inside the house Jack suddenly cried out. For a second – no more – Hal turned his head towards the sound. When he looked back at the garden, the creature had gone. If it had ever been there.

Stiff and cold, Hal uncurled himself, got up from the chair and limped over to the door. No more sound from Jack. Just the murmur of the telly downstairs. Better just see.

He found Jack sound asleep and dreaming, his forehead puckered in a frown, as if trying to solve some weighty problem. Hal tiptoed away and left him to it.

Thirteen

Next morning Hal tried to take his mind off things by tidying up his room. He'd got as far as taking all the books off the shelf, prior to rearranging them. Come to think of it, this was as far as he ever got. As soon as he began sorting through them, something would catch his eye and he'd start reading and before he knew it, it would be dinner-time – just time to bundle them back on the shelf all anyhow, which was really the way he liked them.

Then Ellie stuck her head round the door. 'Dolph Stittle wants you,' she said.

'Dolph? Where?'

'Down by the shed.'

Outside, it was the sort of day that made him feel quite glad after all that he was living in the country.

Fresh air. Warm sun. In the town it would be dusty and sticky as the day went on.

Behind the shed, leaning against the fence with his legs stretched out in front of him, Dolph sat, deep in his book. But not so deep that he didn't notice the movement of Hal's shadow on the ground beside him.

'Good book,' he said, keeping his finger on the page, ready to go on reading. 'I brought the other one back.' He reached inside his shirt for *Viking's Dawn* and handed it to Hal over the fence without getting up.

Was that it? Was that all he wanted?

'Me grandad sent me,' he said. 'He's going to see your gran again today. He thought you might have something you wanted taking to her.'

'Thanks,' said Hal. 'But Mum or Dad will be going . . .'

'Something special,' Dolph interrupted. 'Something to remind her who she really is. He said you'd know. He told me to wait.' He settled down with his book again, prepared to sit there all day if he had to.

Hal wandered back up to the house, wondering what Mr Stittle meant. You couldn't take two steps indoors without catching sight of something that belonged to Gran: ornaments and books, her needlework table, her spinning-wheel . . . They all held little bits of Gran's life.

Upstairs he could hear voices. Mum and Ellie. Ellie seemed to have given up sending Mum to Coventry in favour of a good row.

'You'd got no right!' said Ellie. 'They're not yours to throw away.'

'You can't have them here. Not after they've been in the dustbin.'

'*I* didn't put them in the dustbin.'

'No, I did. And they're going straight back there.'

Gran's pictures. Of course! Hal raced up the stairs, flung himself between Mum and Ellie, so that they both, for a moment, loosened their grip. ' 'Scuse me!' he said, grabbed the pictures and was off down the stairs again.

A thin plume of smoke above the roof of the garden shed showed that Dolph was still there.

'Smoking's bad for you,' Hal observed.

'Tobacco's bad for you,' Dolph corrected him amiably. 'This stuff's OK. Keeps the flies away a treat. Are those what I've got to take?'

Hal looked at the pictures. From under the glass,

Gran's bright eyes smiled back at him, willing him to set her free.

Dolph took them. He said, 'Grandad said you've got the makings of a cunning man.'

'Oh,' said Hal. 'Is that good?'

'Depends on your point of view,' said Dolph. He reflected a moment. 'Yeah. I'd say that's a pretty good thing to be.'

As Dolph turned to go, Hal saw a movement in the undergrowth, like some large animal. Then the twins rose together out of the long grasses, both grinning broadly.

'You never saw us, did you?'

'Even our Dolph, he didn't see us!'

'Take no notice of 'em,' Dolph advised. 'Comes of being twins, you see. They've only got one brain between the two of them.'

Both twins immediately went for him. Dustin punched him sociably in the ribs, while Harrison aimed a swipe at his head. With a skill born of long practice, Dolph somehow managed to dodge both of them, while holding Gran's pictures out of harm's way.

'Watch it!' he warned them. 'Or Grandad'll put the Eye on you!'

The twins subsided, looked round for fresh entertainment and spotted Ellie coming from the house.

'Coo, she looks mad!' muttered Dustin.

'Rather you than me, boy!' Harrison winked at Hal. 'Hi, Ellie!'

'How you doin'?' Dustin enquired.

Ellie had no time to waste on social chitchat. 'What's Dolph Stittle doing with Gran's pictures?' she demanded.

'He's taking them to Gran,' said Hal.

'Oh, yes?' said Ellie, disbelieving.

'Me grandad is,' said Dolph. 'He'll see she gets 'em.'

'You on for tonight, then?' asked Dustin.

'Tonight?' Hal repeated. 'What's happening tonight?'

'The badgers.'

'Didn't we say?'

'Rutger sent us to tell you.'

'Like I said,' put in Dolph, 'no more than half a brain.'

The twins gave him a catch-you-later glare and carried on.

'We're gonna rescue them tonight!'

'You know where they are?' asked Hal.

'Not right this minute, no.'

'We know where they're goin' to be.'

'Tonight.'

'Like we said.'

'You on?'

'I —' Hal wasn't quite sure what he was letting himself in for.

'We're on,' said Ellie.

'At sunset, right?'

'We'll pick you up here.'

'At sunset,' Hal repeated. How long after sunset till it got dark? Not long enough.

'Wear something dark,' Harrison advised them.

'And a balaclava, if you got one,' added Dustin.

Sunset. Obstacles rose up in Hal's mind, not just fear of the dark. There was Mum, too. How to get out of the house without her knowing. How to make sure she didn't find them gone and start phoning the police or something.

'That's if you wanta come,' said Dustin, seeing the hesitation in his face.

'You don't have to, if you don't want,' said Harrison, off-handedly. 'We just thought we'd ask.'

'We can manage without you.'

'You will come, won't you?' Dolph urged him. 'It'll be good!'

'We're coming,' said Ellie firmly. 'See you at sunset.'

'See you later,' grinned Dolph.

The Stittles turned away and the common swallowed them up. Perhaps things weren't so bad, Hal reflected, if Gran had the Stittles fighting her corner – and they could free the badgers, wherever they were.

In the kitchen Mum was sitting alone, moodily stirring a cup of coffee. She didn't look up as they went past. Hal had the impression she might have been crying. If so, she didn't want anyone to know.

In the living-room, Dad and Frank Finnegan were engrossed in a new toy. A camcorder. Dad held it up, scanning the room and the street beyond, then dropped his arms again.

'I'm still not sure about this, Frank,' he said.

'Look, Dan,' said Frank, 'all you have to do is point the damn thing and keep it running. No one's even going to see you. I'll be the one taking all the risks. But we can't rely on them letting me take all the pictures I want.'

'It'll be dark.'

'That's why I brought the night-sight. No problem. I need this, Dan! I need *you*.' There was an edge to Frank's voice Hal had never heard before. Then he turned and saw them. Suddenly he was his usual cheerful self. 'Do you see your dad moving into motion pictures?'

'Not really,' Hal began.

But Frank had already turned away: 'Look, why don't we take it over to Miss Letty's and try it out? I've got to drop in there anyway, for the key.'

'Right. So long as I'm back for lunch. Ba's a stickler for one o'clock Sunday lunch.'

'Fair enough.'

Evening came at last. Dad was out again with Frank Finnegan. That was good. He was far more likely than Mum to come barging in after they'd gone to bed, especially if Hal said he was going up early to read. Mum was watching some detective thing on television.

As soon as it started, Ellie made a great show of yawning and stretching, ending in, 'I think I'll go to bed now. School tomorrow!'

'I think I'll go up, too,' said Hal. 'Read my book for a bit.'

Mum kissed them goodnight, a bit miffed that neither of them had begged to be allowed to stay up and watch with her.

As the sun was going down, Ellie, silent as a ghost, appeared at Hal's bedroom door and beckoned to him. From downstairs came the sound of car engines revving and the squeal of breaks as one of the evening's car chases got under way.

Out of her bedroom window slid Ellie, with a faint crunching of grit as she landed on the roof of the utility room. After her went Hal, more quietly, turning to push the window as near shut as he could. Through the open kitchen window he could still hear the television. Suddenly, the pounding theme music of the film gave way to a merry jingle. The commercials.

Hal froze with his hand still holding the window, while Ellie raised a finger unneccessarily to her lips. If Mum was going to make a move, she'd do it now. His ears strained for the sound of footsteps on the stairs. Then the light went on in the kitchen. It stayed on. The pounding theme music began again, so Mum must be heading back to the living-room.

Silently they agreed to risk it, climbing down via the coal bunker, first Ellie, then Hal, stepping into the shaft of light from the kitchen, resisting a mad urge to turn and take a bow, like an actor entering on stage. Then he was running after Ellie, down the garden, into the welcoming shadows, up the rockery and over the fence. Together they crouched behind the shed, out of breath and giggling with relief.

There was no sign of life on the common, apart from a lone jogger in the distance. Sunday evening in Laxworth. A time to stay home, put your feet up and save your strength for Monday morning.

A soft whistle sounded from somewhere close at hand. A figure rose up out of the undergrowth. Beckoned. And sank out of sight again. After one last glance back at the house, they made their way towards it.

They found the Stittles crouched in a hollow, surrounded by a tangle of blackthorn, wild roses and ragged-Robin. The boys wore balaclavas. Madonna's head was swathed in a black and white checked scarf, like an Arab terrorist. Michelle, in a very fetching Breton sailor's cap, had tied a black silk scarf over her mouth and nose. There was still no mistaking the Stittles.

'I brought you a spare,' said a voice beside Hal. Dolph handed him a khaki balaclava that smelt as if it had been rescued from the dog's basket.

'What about her?' asked Michelle.

Ellie took out a bobble hat. 'Will this do?' she asked.

Michelle took it, sized it up, bit through one of the stitches and pulled until she'd made a big enough gap to see through. 'It'll do,' she said.

The bobble on top looked a bit out of place, but Hal decided not to mention it.

'Right,' said Rutger. 'Let's get going.'

'Where to?' Ellie wanted to know.

'It's Sunday, isn't it?' said Rutger. 'We're going to church.'

Hal fell into line behind Dolph, with the twins behind. Led by Rutger, they wound their way in single file along almost invisible tracks and through what looked from the outside like impenetrable thickets in what did seem to be the general direction of Laxworth Church. Suddenly Rutger stopped, holding up his hand as a signal to the rest to do the same. Miraculously they managed it without anyone cannoning into anybody else.

Rutger sniffed the air. 'Someone followin' us,' he announced.

As one man, the Stittles dived for cover. Hal

found himself sprawling in a patch of wild garlic as the sound of pounding feet came nearer. Whoever it was seemed to be making no attempt to hide themselves. Through the long grasses he glimpsed the jogger he'd seen earlier – dark track suit and baseball cap, a mobile phone sticking out of his pocket, some workaholic fitness freak – then the man was past, with no sign of having seen them, or that he'd been expecting to see them.

False alarm.

They picked themselves up out of the undergrowth, reformed the column and resumed their march, Hal miserably aware that the smell of dog from his balaclava was now quite overpowered by the stink of garlic.

Fourteen

Laxworth Church stood about a mile from the village, all alone on a small hill, hemmed in by shrubs. Once upon a time, the lords of the manor used to stroll down the garden, through a wicket gate and along a path through the woods to church. But the path was all overgrown now with brambles and nettles. Miss Letty used the road like everyone else when she went to put flowers on the altar for the service held there every third Sunday.

Behind the church, the old graveyard sloped unevenly away to a battered flint wall that separated it from the common. As they drew nearer, the church stood out dark and lifeless against the twilit sky. But in the graveyard behind, well hidden from the road, there were lights and movement.

As they drew closer, the column split up. It was

every man for himself. Hal followed the example of the Stittles, picking out each bit of cover in advance, then making a dash for it, crouching low. If he'd stopped to think about it, he'd have had to admit he was actually enjoying himself.

They heard the growl of a car labouring up the steep track to the church from the road. They saw the headlights sweep across the front of the building. Then the engine and lights were doused together and Hal realised, by contrast, how the shadows had thickened around them as they walked. He could hear voices now, a dull murmur of not one, but several conversations.

In the shelter of a clump of bushes not five metres from the wall, they gathered again to take stock. From here they could see into the churchyard. Someone had made a bonfire of the garden rubbish piled over by the far wall. It cast strange, flickering lights over the gravestones and the tombs, so that it was hard to see which were shadows and which were men. The men were drinking from cans, talking in small groups. Some had dogs with them, some muzzled, all on leads.

'There must be dozens of them!' whispered Hal.

'No more'n twenty, I'd say,' said Rutger.

'What are they all doing here?' asked Hal.

'Come for the billy-baiting.'

'Billy —?' In Hal's book, billies meant goats.

'Badgers,' Dolph translated.

Rutger cast an expert eye over the scene. 'Reckon they got them in that blue van. Over the far side. See?'

Hal's heart skipped a beat. 'All of them?'

Rutger shook his head. 'They'll be keeping the cubs somewhere else. They use 'em for training the dogs.'

Hal risked another look, long enough to make out a few faces. Rambo and the Terminator. Polly Froggett with two of his dogs in tow. No surprises there.

'It's like a rave,' Michelle explained. 'People come from all over. They all know *when* it's going to happen. But not where. Not till the last minute, see?'

'So no one who's not s'posed to know finds out,' put in Dolph.

'That's why we had to wait until they'd got it all set up.'

'We'd got no way of knowing where they were keeping them.'

'Now all we've got to do is get 'em out of there.'

Hal risked another glance at the scene in the churchyard. When the Stittles talked about rescuing the badgers under cover of darkness, he'd imagined nothing more dangerous than a bit of quiet breaking and entering into a shed or a barn somewhere. His courage was ebbing fast as he thought about what they were taking on. A bunch of vicious killers. Kids against grown-ups. Outnumbered by more than two to one. The Stittles had to be insane.

'Best get moving,' said Rutger. 'We haven't got much time.' The other Stittles obediently straightened their balaclavas and began moving off into the shadows. Rutger turned to Hal and Ellie. 'You two stay here, right? You're our reserve.'

Hal nodded, quite content to be a reserve, but not so Ellie. No sooner had Rutger melted away into the gathering dark than she was moving forward towards the wall.

'Ellie!' But his voice was less than a whisper. There was nothing for it but to go after her.

'I didn't just come to watch,' said Ellie, as he joined her in the shelter of the wall.

'There's nothing we can do, Ellie. The Stittles are a team. And we're the reserve. What happens if Rutger comes back and we're not there?'

'He's not coming back. You know that.'

'OK. Fine.'

'You know what you are, Hal Cornish? You're a wimp!'

Hal risked a quick glance over the wall and thought he saw a small shadow dart between one tombstone and another. Most of the action was out of his line of sight, blocked by the Harding family vault. It was as big as a garage, with wrought-iron gates and life-size angels at the corners.

Minutes went by. Ellie had her sulking head on.

Above the general buzz of conversation, two voices seemed to detach themselves from the rest. A man and a girl in bikers' gear, arms around each other, were strolling towards the wall.

'Quick, Ellie! We've got to move.'

'Why?'

'Just do it!'

They scrambled along the length of the wall until they reached the end, where the flints gave way to a double strand of wire. They crawled through and, at Ellie's insistence, began making their way forward again, dodging between the gravestones. At one point they barely made it into cover as a man and a dog appeared from the direction where the cars were parked. The dog pulled eagerly to where they crouched, but the man dragged it away and walked on, then stopped again and fell into conversation with another man who spoke with a thick, Irish accent.

'Tom Parker, isn't it?' said the Irishman.

'That's right,' came the reply. 'Er —?'

'Doyle. You remember, I was asking about . . . Is this the little bitch, then?'

'I wouldn't come too close, if I was you. She's ready to go.'

'I can see she's game. By the scars.'

'You won't see a set of medals to beat 'em. Won a cup for those, she did.'

'And the pups?'

'Three left. All good 'uns.'

'Could be just what my brother's looking for. Would you mind if I took a few pictures? So he can see how she looks in action?'

'Take all you want. Just the dog, mind.'

'I'll keep you out of them, don't worry. What about the father?'

'Dead, a couple of weeks back. Had him working a sett over Melford way. Old Brocky came out fighting. Took half his jaw away. Had to shoot him. No choice.'

'A game 'un, then.'

'Yeah.'

'Right. Catch you later.'

The man with the dog moved away and the Irishman stopped to light a cigarette. As the match flared up, they saw his face.

'Frank Finnegan!' Ellie exclaimed. 'He *is* one of them!'

If she had said any other name, Frank would never have heard her. But there's something about hearing your own name spoken, even very softly. Frank Finnegan froze as if someone had suddenly pointed a gun at his head. He peered uncertainly into the darkness, then slowly began to move towards them.

Hal and Ellie crouched motionless behind the gravestone. There was nothing else they could do. He was bound to see them if they moved. It wasn't until he was standing beside them that they realised he'd seen them from way back. He was still peering into the dark beyond, when he suddenly reached down and yanked them to their feet.

'I *knew* you were one of them!' Ellie burst out.

'Ellie?' demanded Frank, gripping her harder. 'So this must be Hal. What in the name of blue blazes are you two doing here?' The thick Irish accent was gone, so, too, was the hail-fellow-well-met Frank Finnegan always inviting himself to tea.

'Wouldn't you like to know?' taunted Ellie.

'Where's Dad?' Hal asked suddenly. Surely Dad was supposed to be out on a job with Frank Finnegan tonight.

'Not here,' said Frank, but he couldn't keep his eyes from glancing briefly towards the church tower.

'He's up there, isn't he?' said Ellie. 'What have you done with him?'

'Ellie, don't be daft,' Hal protested weakly.

But Ellie was dragging all three of them towards the tower. Rather than draw attention to them, Frank let himself be pulled along while he tried to reason with her. 'Your dad's OK, Ellie. I give you my word. Will you just go home now, the pair of you? Can't you persuade her, Hal?'

There was the sound of footsteps on gravel. 'Get out of sight!' hissed Frank.

The two of them crouched behind a buttress while Frank stood in front, pretending to light his already lit cigarette. He nodded and murmured a greeting to the two men who passed. Then he turned and knocked on the door at the base of the tower: dee-dee-dee-dah, like the victory sign during the war. After a few moments, they heard the big key turn in the lock. The door opened a crack and they heard Dad's startled voice: 'Oh, my godfathers! What are you two doing here?' Balaclavas or not, he knew his own children.

'Just keep them out of sight, Dan, will you?' snapped Frank.

Hal felt a hand in the small of his back, pushing him stumbling through the door after Ellie. Dad closed it behind them and turned the key. It was almost pitch-dark inside the church, but they didn't need to see his face to know that he was angry. Angry and frightened.

'Does your mother know you're out?'

Hal shook his head.

'We came to save the —' Ellie began.

'I don't care why you came,' snapped Dad. The fact that he was whispering, not shouting, only made it worse. 'It was stupid! Stupid and dangerous. Come with me.'

They followed him in silence up the spiral stairway of the tower. The stone was worn and slippery underfoot and there was nothing to hold on to but an old piece of rope. About halfway up the tower they came to a narrow landing with a boarded floor and an unglazed, double-arched window which gave a good view over the graveyard.

Among the grassy dips and hummocks lay one depression much deeper and wider than the rest, where a wartime bomb had fallen. The people of Laxworth had used the hole for a rubbish dump until it was almost full to the top, then bulldozed in some earth and grassed it over. But that hole seemed to eat rubbish. Each year it sagged deeper, forming a natural arena. Now straw bales had been placed round it, except where the blue van Rutger pointed out had been backed up to the edge.

Hal looked in vain for any sign of the Stittles. They were leaving things a bit late. Men and dogs were beginning to converge on the circle. Two of the men at least were armed with baseball bats. Another, carrying a rifle, climbed on to one of the stone tombs and sat with the gun balanced across his knees. Where were the Stittles?

'You know what's going on?' said Dad.

Hal nodded, his throat too dry to speak.

'I'm afraid you're going to be stuck here till it's over. My advice is, don't watch. Go down into the church and wait for me there. And take those silly

206

hats off. You must be roasting.' He picked up the camcorder and turned to the window.

'You're going to film it?' said Ellie.

'You heard me, Ellie. Get down into the church, both of you.'

'But aren't you going to do anything to stop it?' Ellie insisted.

'We're going to try and stop it happening again. To do that, I have to film it. Get the evidence.'

'If you let one badger die, then you're as bad as those men down there.'

'Ellie, I haven't got time to argue. Can't you – just this once – do as you're told?'

Ellie was opening her mouth to speak again when there came a hideous sound from somewhere outside, wailing, unearthly. It was no more than a note or two, but Hal felt the hair on the back of his neck standing on end. Then the sound was blotted out, as one of the dogs began to howl, and went on howling.

From the window, Hal could see it, one of a pair. It just sat there, howling, while its partner ran backwards and forwards at the limit its lead would allow, looking for the source of that dreadful keening. Several other dogs were getting restive.

One or two began to howl in sympathy, despite all their owners could do to shut them up as they scanned the darkness, looking for where the noise was coming from.

Each time the dog took a breath, the wailing could still be heard. Gradually the men tracked it. Heads turned towards the Harding family tomb, ears straining to make sure. But as soon as two of them took a step towards it, the sound abruptly stopped. The dog stopped howling. Men began to relax, still throwing curious glances towards the tomb. An effect of the wind, perhaps? Maybe.

Then the sound began again, from a completely different direction, somewhere out on the common. A different note. A different dog affected – no, two this time, which made the source harder to pin down. But in the split second before they began Hal recognised the sound for what it was.

A mouth organ! Two mouth organs. Owned by the twins. They had pulled a similar trick at school once, nearly driving the history teacher wild until he found out he wasn't the only person who could hear it.

None of the men was looking at the blue van. None of them saw what Hal could see from where he stood at the window: a shadow, darker than the rest, moving silently along the dark side of the van. Dolph? No, taller: it must be Rutger.

Reaching the rear corner of the van, he cast a fearful glance around, before stretching out an arm into the light to try the handle on the rear doors. They were locked. He started back again, towards the driver's door – looking to see if the key to the rear doors was in the ignition? He never made it.

Whatever small sound the rattling of the handle had made, someone at the back of the crowd had heard it and realised something was up. Swift and silent as a cat, a figure leapt, caught hold of Rutger by the collar, twisted his left arm up behind him and half-dragged, half-carried him back to the rest. He whisked off the balaclava and with the help of another man, Rutger was hoisted up on to the nearest tomb.

One of them bunched up his fist and yelled above the noise, 'Stop that racket, or he gets it!'

The noise stopped. The dogs fell silent. So did the men.

The twisted arm must be hurting like fury, but Rutger stood up to them. 'I only came to watch,' he scowled. 'It's all right if I watch, isn't it?' he appealed to the men standing round.

'What were you doing by the van?'

'Just looking. I never saw a brocky close to.'

'Who's that out there?'

'The twins. They were just mucking about. You know the twins. They must've followed me.'

'Anyone else follow you?'

'Oh, yes! I thought I might as well bring the whole family while I was about it. And one or two friends. They're all out there somewhere.'

'Shut 'im up!'

Then one of the older men stepped forward. 'Let him go,' he said quietly. 'Stittles don't grass, do they, son?' Rutger shook his head. 'Best way to make sure,' went on the man, 'is let him stay. He won't grass himself up, will he?' There were murmurs of agreement. 'So let him go,' said Rutger's new-found friend. 'We're wasting time.'

Reluctantly, the two men let Rutger go, though not without an extra twist to his arm from one and a sly clip round the ear from the other. The crowd turned back to the main business of the evening.

That was when Hal noticed Ellie was missing. She must have gone down into the church, as Dad had told them to do. Hal felt his way down the stairs to join her. But as soon as he stepped into the main part of the church, he knew there was no one else there.

He checked up and down the rows of pews. There was enough light coming from outside to see she wasn't down by the font or up by the altar, or even (a last resort) hiding in the pulpit. He went back to the door at the bottom of the tower and tried it. The door was unlocked. Ellie must be somewhere outside.

Fifteen

Outside, this side of the church was in pitch darkness. Just around the corner, the spotlights made it as bright as day. He could tell from the noise that the evening's entertainment was getting under way.

The Stittles had failed. He'd put such faith in them and they'd failed. He told himself it wasn't their fault. What could a bunch of kids do against so many? The thing now was to find Ellie. Find her, before she got herself into real trouble.

He tried to shut his ears to the snarling of the dogs, the shouts of the crowd, egging them on . . . a sudden shriek of pain, almost like a baby's cry. His eyes scanned the hummocks of the graves and the ancient tombstones, half-buried in the earth, lopsided, like so many lurking figures. Ellie could be anywhere among them. All she had to do was crouch down and keep still. He'd never spot her. Then he saw Michelle.

Dressed head to foot in black, she would have been invisible, if it hadn't been for the creature with her. Its silver-grey fur gleamed in the soft overspill of the lights. He recognised the creature of his nightmares, the creature of his dreams. A few steps forward and he'd be able to touch it and know it was real. The wolf. But there are no wolves in England. Not any more. Hal stood and watched, spellbound.

Michelle was crouching with one arm round the wolf's neck, her head bent close, talking softly into its ear. She'd pulled her scarf down below her chin. Hal could see her lips move, but he couldn't hear what she said. She rubbed her cheek gently against its fur. The wolf turned his head and licked her nose in a soft, doggy way. Then he fixed his gaze on the circle of men round the arena. Michelle gave him a final pat and stood up. Her lips formed the single word: 'Now!'

From a standing start, the wolf seemed to reach something close to light speed in no seconds flat, gathered itself and sprang for the backs of the cheering crowd, tearing a path straight through them and landing in the arena beyond. Two of the men were knocked sideways in its onward rush. One saved himself by clutching at the straw bales. The other crashed headlong into the fight between dogs and badger. Through the gap they left, Hal had a glimpse of the wolf as it turned to face the crowd, teeth bared, head low, and the stunned faces of the men opposite as they instinctively fell back.

He couldn't tell what happened next: whether the wolf attacked the dogs; the dogs went for the man on the ground, while someone tried to haul them off; or whether wolf and badger stood shoulder to shoulder, fending off all comers. Pandemonium seemed to break out everywhere at once. Dogs began barking, scrapping with one another, snapping at any stray leg, dog or human, that came within range. Men kicked and swore.

The men who held the dogs had all their attention taken up with trying to control them, while the rest milled around, shouted, swore and snatched up stones and branches to defend themselves. Only one person kept his head. Rutger broke away from the mêlée and headed straight for the blue van.

Standing on his stone tomb, the man with the rifle was trying to get a clear shot at the creature that was causing all the trouble. Before he had a chance, Madonna sprang and clamped herself to his back like the Old Man of the Sea, with her hands firmly over his eyes. He swung backwards and forwards trying to shake her off, but she was like a limpet.

And the blue van was on the move, with its back doors swinging open, weaving a path between the gravestones, bumping over the graves, as it turned in a wide arc. Men and dogs scattered out of its path. It left behind a gap in the circle of straw bales which the twins rushed to widen, making a clear path for the badger's escape. They danced up and down and clapped their hands, urging it in the right direction and Hal cheered aloud as he saw it break free of the circle and make towards the cover of the bushes.

Perched on top of the flint wall, Dolph, the family arsonist, brandished a discarded beer bottle and threw it hard. It smashed against a gravestone and exploded in a sheet of flame, causing still more mayhem.

Through it all the blue van bumpily emerged, gathering speed towards the path that led down to the road. As it lurched past him, Hal caught sight of Rutger's face, triumphant, at the wheel. The van skidded on the gravel. Righted itself. Then it was gone.

Another sheet of flame leapt up from among the straw bales. Silhouetted against it, Hal saw a man running straight towards him, closing fast. He looked round in panic for a way of escape. Then he heard Frank Finnegan's voice: 'They're on to me, Hal!' He felt the camera thrust into his hands. 'It's all in there. The evidence we need. Take it and run!'

Hal started off and saw his way blocked almost at once by a man swinging a baseball bat. He ducked to avoid it. Tripped. Fell. Rolled. Then he was up again and running. Ducking and weaving among the gravestones. He could sense the man still on his track, but falling behind, too big and heavy for this kind of slalom.

Up on the wall Dolph brandished another firebomb ready to throw, choosing his target.

'Dolph! Help me!'

Dolph swung to face him and lobbed the bottle over Hal's head. Hal felt the surge of heat behind him, saw his own shadow stretch out in front, curving away over the wall. He followed it. He heard the crack of a rifle as he hit the ground, but he'd made it!

This is the bit where the hero runs through the dark, clear-sighted as a cat, sure-footed as a goat, outrunning and out-smarting his pursuers. But Hal didn't feel like a hero. Tussocks of grass seemed to spring up on purpose to trip him. Brambles caught at his clothes. Nettles stung him. Gorse scratched him. Branches swung down to bar his way.

He soon had no idea which way he was heading. He was making so much noise, he couldn't tell if anyone was still on his trail. He risked a quick glance behind, but before he could register anything but looming shadows and sky, he caught his foot in a root and fell sprawling.

He felt a sharp stab at his ankle as the root reluctantly let go, followed by a sickening pain in his ribs from a stone lurking under the bed of leaves that cushioned the worst of his fall. Miraculously, he was still holding on to Frank's camera.

He lay there, winded, ears pricked for any sound of pursuit. The night air was full of noises. Creeping and rustling. Even the fallen leaves seemed to stir with invisible life . . . A sudden sharp cry! What was it? A fox? An owl startled him, swooping low overhead on silent wings. It came to rest on a branch not far off. He could sense, rather than see it, staring at him, sizing him up, before gliding off into the dark again, in search of something better to eat.

Lying here among the leaves, the night slowly lost its terrors. It was almost like lying in bed. Why shouldn't he just lie here until morning? If they came looking . . . He remembered a film he'd seen where the hero managed to hide himself in open ground in broad daylight by covering himself with grass and leaves. After a few minutes' scrabbling, Hal decided it just wasn't possible, not in real life.

Then he heard them. Men's voices, some distance to his left, and the sound of bodies moving through the undergrowth. A shout! Someone had found his track. Then they were on the move again, coming closer.

Wearily he got to his feet. He winced as he put his weight on the damaged ankle. Which way should he go? Which way? He'd no idea. But the common didn't go on for ever. Whichever way he travelled, so long as he kept in a straight line, he was bound to come to a road, lights, people . . .

He'd forgotten about Dead Man's Pool. Roughly in the middle of the common it lay, dark and menacing. People who bought houses on the new estate had tried to get the council to drain it. Locals shook their heads and said it was impossible: the pool was bottomless. The surface lay so still in the moonlight and the sedge clustered so thickly round the edge that before he realised it, he'd blundered in right up to his knees, thick mud dragging at his shoes. With some difficulty he turned – each time he managed to drag one foot out, the other was sucked deeper in – and made his way to the edge.

He heard something approaching fast through the undergrowth, travelling low – too low for a man. One of the dogs, maybe, freelancing? The sedge in front of him parted and he found himself face to face with the wolf.

They stood staring at one another, their faces on a level, both unsure what to do next. The wolf was panting slightly, tongue hanging out, sharp teeth showing bone-white in the moonlight. It gave a soft growl, deep in its throat, but it didn't attack. It was more as if it was trying to say hello. Hal had a stupid desire to giggle. Then he heard the sounds of pursuit again, much closer.

'Shoo!' whispered Hal, flapping his free hand feebly towards the wolf. 'Get away! You'll lead them to me. Shoo!'

The creature stared at him, an expression close to a smile on its face.

'Shoo. Please, shoo.'

It seemed to understand. Even gave a little nod of its head, before backing carefully away, so the sedge looked undisturbed. A few moments later, he heard a shout, and an answering cry, the crack of a rifle. And the hunt was on! – but in quite the wrong direction.

They were soon far enough away to make Hal feel safe to scramble out of Dead Man's Pool and on to dry land again. Cold water and mud had done his ankle good, if anything. The pain had dulled to a persistent ache, no worse when he put his weight on it. Which way now? The darkness closed in on him all around and he began to shiver.

All right, he told himself. You can stay here and be frightened. Or you can keep on the move and you might get out before morning. Right. Which way, then?

He looked in vain for some landmark that would tell him where he was. He might have walked halfway round the pool in the dark before wandering back towards it and blundering in. No sign of light anywhere. Someone must have doused the fires up at the church. Only the moon and the stars.

The stars! Of course, you could navigate by the stars. Find the North Star, and you'd be all right. There was the Plough . . . and the Pointers . . . so that was north. The faintest glow of light on the horizon confirmed it: the town of Melford with its streetlamps was due north of Laxworth. The common lay between, roughly north and east of the village.

Hal turned west and set off. Oh, but he was dog-tired now . . . A movement ahead and to his right snapped him awake again. He changed his course slightly to the left in order to avoid it. When he looked up at the sky again to check his direction, he found he was still heading due west. Twice more this happened. Someone – something – was guiding him the way he had to go. Why didn't it show itself? Was it the wolf? *So this is how the sheep feels at a sheepdog trial.*

Then there were smooth stones underfoot. A cobbled path, much overgrown with weeds and brambles, but still a path. It must lead somewhere. He checked the stars again and turned right. As he followed the path along, he could hear the wolf – if it was the wolf – keeping pace with him among the undergrowth. Why didn't it show itself? Perhaps it didn't want to frighten him.

The path ended at a brick wall, too high to see over, and a gate, bolted on the far side. Hal shook the handle, rattled it and pushed with all his might, but the bolt held fast. He could have cried.

Then he saw the wolf's grey shape emerge from the woods further along the wall. It cast up and down parallel to the wall. As it went, Hal could see that the ground below, under the tangle of weeds, was nowhere near as level as it seemed to be. The wolf turned towards him again and he saw a dark stain at its shoulder. Blood. He noticed now that it was limping slightly. That last shot he'd heard must have found its mark. The wolf chose the place where the bank was highest, sprang for the top of the wall and dragged itself over.

Where he goes, thought Hal, I should be able to go, too. No sense in standing here.

Fingers on the top of the wall, he scrabbled with his feet, finding toeholds in the crumbling brick, enough to help him up. Stretched out on the top of the wall he paused, resting, taking in the scene. Neatly trimmed lawns and flowerbeds. The irregular shape of a large house. And a light in one of the downstairs rooms.

On the lawn, the wolf stood patiently waiting and trotted beside him as he made his way towards the light. Near by was a door. He knocked. And the door was opened. Light and warmth spilled out from a well-scrubbed kitchen.

'Hal Cornish!' exclaimed Miss Letty's voice. 'However did you get here?'

Sixteen

Hal glanced back across the lawn. The wolf had faded away into moonlight and shadows. He felt suddenly sick and there was a ringing in his ears that seemed to come from far, far away.

'Come in and sit down,' said Miss Letty.

The door closed behind him and he allowed himself to be led to a big, wheel-backed chair, its seat plump with cushions.

'Sit down,' she said, 'and put your head between your knees.'

He did as he was told. The kitchen floor came slowly into focus. It was tiled red and black, like a chessboard, and smelt strongly of disinfectant.

The ringing in his ears faded and he heard Miss Letty clearly. 'You have been in the wars, haven't you? Can you sit up now? Let's have a look at you.'

He saw that, although it must be well past midnight, she was fully dressed.

'Hot, sweet tea!' she said suddenly.

'Huh?'

'Hot, sweet tea, that's what you need. I'll put the kettle on. I used to drive an ambulance during the war. The ladies of the WVS were always there ahead of us, dishing out gallons of hot, sweet tea.'

Hal didn't feel up to arguing that he didn't really like tea.

'I would offer you a hot bath,' she said, 'but the tank takes an age to heat up. You'll just have to dunk your feet in a bowl of hot water. So let's get these shoes off. Oh! What's this?'

His left ankle was swollen to twice its normal size.

Miss Letty examined it with expert fingers, pressing gently. 'Tell me if I hurt you.' She eased the foot from side to side and up and down. 'Hm. I'm fairly sure it's not broken,' she decided. 'Though you should get it X-rayed to be on the safe side. I've got a crêpe bandage upstairs. That will make it more comfortable. Any more war wounds?'

Hal pointed to his ribs.

'Roll up your shirt. Let's see. My goodness, that's quite a bruise. How did you do that?'

'I fell on a stone, I think.'

'Could be a cracked rib or two. Not much I can do for that. I'll fetch the bandage for your ankle. You'd better get out of those wet trousers, too. You can borrow my dressing-gown to keep you decent.'

The dressing gown was long and heavy as an overcoat, designed for a house with no central heating. He had trouble getting his arm into the sleeve until Miss Letty said, 'I think you could put this down now.'

He found he was still clutching Frank Finnegan's camera.

'I'll put it on the table,' she said. 'So you can keep an eye on it.'

Miss Letty didn't fuss. She did what needed to be done, no more, no less. He slid his feet into the bowl of soothing water and sipped his hot, sweet tea gratefully when it came. He still didn't like the taste, but it did make him feel comfortably warm inside.

'Now,' she said, 'perhaps you're ready to tell me what you're doing tearing around the countryside at this hour.'

He tried to get his thoughts into some sort of order, but his brain was tired and just wanted to be left alone.

'Shall we begin with the camera?' she suggested. 'It's small, but expensive. I don't think it's yours. So who does it belong to?'

'Frank Finnegan,' said Hal. 'He gave it to me to look after.'

'When? Tonight?'

Hal hesitated. She seemed like someone you could rely on, someone you could trust, but . . .

'Would it help,' she asked gently, 'if I were to tell you what I know already?' She knelt down and began gently drying his feet. 'Poor Mr Finnegan, with his cunning plan for getting into my niece's house so he could snoop around. I could tell at once that he wasn't interested in my house or me. But once he'd made up his mind to be honest with me, I decided a little help wouldn't come amiss.'

She wound the crêpe bandage round his foot and ankle in a neat criss-cross pattern. 'It seems he's been on the track of this gang of badger-baiters for some time, gaining their confidence until they trusted him enough to let him take the photographs he needed. He was with them when they dug out the sett over at Melford and took the baby badgers. He was almost certain that my niece's husband was keeping them in the stables. I offered to take a look for him, but that wouldn't have suited Frank Finnegan, Ace Reporter! He had to be able to say he'd done it himself. I believe he's even got a television company interested in the story – which is why he borrowed the camcorder. I made it clear, when he collected the key of the church this afternoon, how strongly I disapproved of his involving your father.'

'I don't think any of them knew Dad was there.'

'Good.'

Hal's mind went back to that chaotic scene in the churchyard: rifle shots and men wielding baseball bats. 'I hope Frank's all right,' he said.

'In my experience,' said Miss Letty, 'the Frank Finnegans of this world are always all right. But whatever possessed your father to take you with him?'

'He didn't. We – I was trying to rescue the badgers.'

'Very commendable. We must let him know that you're safe. The telephone is in the library. Shall we adjourn?'

Hal slipped the camera into the dressing-gown's capacious pocket and followed her out of the kitchen, straight into the great hall of the Manor House. The vastness of it took his breath away, walls towering straight up to the roof, where the beams lost themselves in darkness. All the other rooms led off it. Coconut-matting, laid over stone flags, scratched his bare foot. About half a metre of dressing-gown trailed along the floor after him. He must look like Sweetpea in the Popeye cartoons.

'In here,' said Miss Letty.

Books everywhere, floor to ceiling. Leather chairs.

'You should keep warm,' she said. 'I'll switch on the fire.'

The fireplace was huge and marble. The fire was small and electric. No fake logs. Miss Letty didn't go in for fakes. Hal sat drowsing in one of the shiny leather armchairs, trying not to slide off the edge, while Miss Letty made her phone call. His sleepy eyes roved past her, to a stained-glass window, where some saint or other was preaching to all the races of the world, among them a man with a wolf's head . . .

'Hal! Hal!' Miss Letty was shaking him awake, smiling at him. 'Come on. Let's get you home. You may as well keep my dressing-gown on. I've got a selection of footwear by the door.'

Hal found a pair of sandals to fit over his bandage, then he stood, looking into the darkness, while Miss

Letty fetched the car. He knew he'd never be afraid of the dark again.

Dad must have been listening for them. He had the front door open before they were halfway up the path, launched himself off the step and caught Hal in a massive bear hug that left him gasping for air. It was very un-Dadlike.

'Hal!' he exclaimed. 'You idiot!'

As soon as he could get his head free, Hal glanced nervously past him for signs of Mum. If this was how Dad greeted him after a couple of hours away, he hated to think what Mum's 'welcome home' would be. A ticker-tape parade, perhaps, with the massed bands of the Royal Scots Dragoon Guards?

'Where's Mum?' he asked.

'In bed asleep.' Dad looked a bit shifty. 'You know how hard it is to wake her. And it's not as if there was anything she could do. I thought one of us worrying was enough.' He was looking past Hal, into the darkness. 'Where's Ellie?'

'Isn't she with you?'

Dad shook his head, suddenly worried again.

'I expect she went home with the Stittles,' said Hal.

'Then we should telephone them at once,' said Miss Letty. 'Shall we go inside?'

As soon as they were indoors, Dad grabbed Hal and hugged him again.

'Ouch!' said Hal.

'What's the matter?'

'Possibly a cracked rib or two,' said Miss Letty matter-of-factly. 'Also a sprained ankle. He should be X-rayed. Apart from that, he seems to be quite roadworthy. I'll put the kettle on.'

'Hot, sweet tea,' Hal mouthed at Dad.

Dad smiled at Hal, half-submerged in Miss Letty's dressing-gown. 'You look like Sweetpea.'

'I know,' grinned Hal. 'I'll go and put some clothes on. Oh! You'd better take this.' He took the camera out of his pocket and handed it over.

'Thanks,' said Dad. 'You deserve a medal for hanging on to this.'

'It was no trouble,' Hal said modestly.

'I could have throttled Frank when he told me he'd given it to you. He knew Miss Harding would have phoned the police by then and they'd be on their way.'

'I insisted the police be kept informed,' said Miss Letty. 'After all, I am a magistrate.' She'd found the embroidered cloth Aunt May had brought back from Portugal and was spreading it carefully on the coffee table. 'I was waiting up when you knocked on my door, Hal, expecting them to ring with news of further developments. They searched the stables at my niece's house earlier in the evening and found six badger cubs alive and well. It is against the law to keep wild animals in captivity without a licence.'

'By the time they got to the church,' said Dad, 'there wasn't a badger in sight, but a number of the dogs were in a pretty bad way. That was enough reason to make some arrests. We'll need the pictures of the badger-baiting to get the whole gang. Of course, the police would have got there a bit sooner, if that blue van hadn't nearly run slap-bang into them as it came down the hill.'

'Did they catch it?'

'No way! They were too busy trying to keep out of the ditch.'

Hal grinned to himself as he climbed upstairs, treasuring the memory of Rutger's face as he steered the van through the astonished crowd. Mum's bedroom door was shut, but Hal could hear her breathing deeply, on the brink of snoring. He hurried along to his own room and put on the first clothes that came to hand. Going back towards the stairs, he heard Jack call out.

'Sh!' whispered Hal. 'You'll wake Mum.'

Jack rolled over, grabbed the bars of his cot and hauled himself to his feet. Great! Here was someone to play with at last. So what if it was the middle of the night . . .

'Sh, Jack.' Hal picked him up. After checking to make sure he didn't need changing, he stood rocking the baby gently backwards and forwards.

Already there was enough light in the room to see by. The sun would soon be rising. He carried Jack over to the window and drew the curtains right back. The whole of the eastern sky seemed to be on fire.

'Look at that, Jack! Isn't it beautiful?' Jack clapped his hands.

Was that a shout? A shout from far away across the common. Jack heard it too. His little face was screwed up in a frown, his gaze caught by something. A ripple in the long grass.

'Ellie,' he said suddenly.

'Ellie? Where, Jack? Show me where.' Hal scanned the common, patched still with vast, deep shadows, trying to judge the exact spot Jack had been looking at. Then, far away on the horizon, he saw a flash of light. And another. Figures moving across the common.

'Can you see them, Jack? What's going on? Who are they?' Jack seemed to have lost interest again. He fell to sucking his fingers and twiddling his ear. Hal carried him downstairs.

Dad was standing by the phone. He said, 'The Stittles are doing a head count. They don't think Ellie's with them, but Rutger's not home yet and neither are the twins. Beryl doesn't seem worried. She says they've probably gone to their grandad's and, of course, he's not on the phone. She'll send one of the girls round first thing in the morning. We've phoned the police, too, just in case. If Ellie's not back, they'll organise a search of the common as soon as it's light.'

'I thought I saw people out on the common just now,' said Hal.

'Looking for the Beast of Laxworth, I expect,' Miss Letty said sceptically, coming out of the kitchen. She set down a tray of tea things and began to pour tea into Mum's Sunday-best china cups.

Dad said, 'Miss Harding's a non-believer – but she didn't see what we saw. You saw it, Hal, you must have done. That creature! It moved so fast . . . It was a bit like a big dog.'

'Yes,' said Hal, 'it did look a lot like a dog.'

'I expect that's what it was, then,' said Miss Letty. 'One of their silly dogs. We'll be waiting up, Hal, in case there's news of Eleanor. Why don't you put your little brother back to bed? And come and sit with us?'

Hal nodded. He decided not to mention that Jack might have caught a glimpse of Ellie out on the common. Dad was worried enough already. He carried the baby upstairs. Jack was getting heavy, but not sleepy.

Hal put him down on the window-ledge, which was wide enough to kneel on, and together they watched the dawn. The light was increasing every moment. The blaze of red had thinned out into streaks shot through with every colour from white to purple. Suddenly Jack knelt bolt upright. He seemed to be listening. Hal could hear nothing.

'Where's Ellie, then, Jack? Find Ellie!'

'Ellie!'

With one arm wrapped round Jack to stop him falling, Hal reached over and opened the window. Through the still, cold air he heard a shout, far over to his right. Another answered it. *Ellie?* He tried to let his mind reach out to her, the way it used to do when she was little, picking up the signals of hunger, cold, fear . . .

The crack of a rifle brought him back again. Suddenly he knew! Those flashes of light he'd seen were sunlight reflecting off guns! And Ellie was out there. It was obvious where she'd be, when he thought about it. She'd seen the wolf in the church-yard, and at least one man with a gun. Save the Badgers was history. She was off to save the wolf, ready to fling herself between it and the guns, if she had to!

Jack stirred in his arms and began to whimper.

'I know, Jack. They're hunting him. Hunting him with guns. Don't worry, Jack. He'll be all right.'

Jack gave a determined lurch towards the window.

'Yes, Jack. I think we should go outside, but let's use the door.'

A moment to put a sweater on and wrap the baby in his anorak. Then down the stairs. From the living-room he could hear Miss Letty's voice: 'A nursing home? But that's absurd! She's younger than I am.' He couldn't make out Dad's reply, only Miss Letty again: 'I'm sorry, Daniel. Of course, it may be the best thing after the fright she's had.'

They sat drinking hot, sweet tea, fortified with whisky, Hal noticed as he tiptoed past the door.

'Would you like me to have a chat with her?' Miss Letty went on. 'Find out what she really wants? And she can tell me to my face that I'm an interfering old busybody.'

Outside the morning air struck chill and the dew on his feet even colder. Over to the east, he could see the sun beginning to climb – oh, so slowly – over the horizon. With Jack still in his arms, he scrambled up the rockery.

'Ellie!' he shouted. 'Ellie! This way! Leave him, Ellie! He doesn't need your help.'

Beside him, right in his ear, came an odd crowing noise from Jack, swelling into a blood-curdling howl. *What does the little mouse say, Jack?* But who on earth had taught him to howl like that?

It brought an answering howl from over to the left, towards the shelter of the woods. Further off, and to the right, men's voices were raised, loud and excited. Bodies blundered through the under-growth, cursing at the gorse and nettles getting in their way.

'Ellie!' Jack's sharp eyes had caught a subtler

movement – no more than a sighing of the wind through the grass.

One of the men had seen it too. There was a shout! A single shot. Then a volley of them. And then a terrible cry, more animal than human.

Hal's lips formed the word: 'No!' But no sound came out. *No, no, no!* Jack started to cry.

He didn't remember climbing over the fence. One minute he was standing on the rockery, disbelieving his own ears and then he was moving across the rough ground, nettles stinging his feet, thistles scratching them, Jack still keening in his arms. Ahead of him a barefoot figure in shirt and jeans emerged from the dark background of the woods and moved quickly towards them as Jack gave a joyful cry of recognition. It was Lemmy Stittle, who stopped, looking down at something by his feet.

Behind him, Hal heard Miss Letty, in tones that would have done credit to a Regimental Sergeant-Major: 'Hold your fire! There is a child in there!' There was silence, broken only by the sound of people hurrying towards the spot.

Ellie lay still, her eyes closed. There was blood everywhere. The bullet had lodged in her side, but she seemed to have fallen awkwardly, twisting her leg under her as she went down. Reaching them first, Hal thrust Jack into Lemmy's arms to hold. Automatically, Lemmy went to take him on his left side, as right-handed people do, then at the last minute shifted him to his right.

Hal bent over Ellie and managed to check that she was still breathing before Miss Letty arrived and took charge. 'Don't move her,' she said. 'We must keep her warm. Coats!'

Stunned sportsmen put down their guns and took off their coats and sweaters. 'I never meant —' one of them began.

'Stop blethering and come here,' Miss Letty interrupted him. 'I suppose it's too much to ask if any of you has a clean handkerchief.'

Polly Froggett took off his silk cravat and offered it without a word.

'That will have to do,' she sniffed, folding it into a pad and placing it against the wound in Ellie's side. 'Press firmly on that and keep on pressing, while I check for further injuries. Daniel, go and telephone for an ambulance.'

Hal stood up and looked round for Lemmy. He was standing a little apart, still holding a now very sleepy Jack, seeming not to notice the nettles under his bare feet. A shiver ran down Hal's spine as he realised why they looked so unnaturally long and thin. Lemmy had only four toes on each foot. Just like a wolf.

Somewhere inside his head, he heard Gran's voice, clear as a bell: *nothing to be afraid of.* Except that Gran thought such things could only happen in stories. This was real. Sad eyes gazed at him. Lemmy the simpleton, literally 'not all there'. It was only in the darkness that, like Uncle Ho, he could become truly himself. Bisclavret. Lord of the forest, alive to every sound and scent and shadow in the world around him.

If Hal had needed any more convincing, there was the blood on Lemmy's shirt, seeping through from the shoulder wound made hours before and reopened by the effort when he took hold of Jack.

'I should get someone to look at that shoulder,' Hal said quietly.

'The cunning man,' said Lemmy. 'He'll see to it.'

Hal raised his hand and gently touched the wound. 'It's not as bad as it looks, is it? The bullet went straight through.'

'I'll be all right. You should see to her.'

Hal turned to look at Ellie, still lying deathly still under a mound of coats and sweaters. He heard Miss Letty's voice: 'She may have hit her head when she fell. Or else, jarred her spine so badly . . .'

She was worried, Hal could tell. He knelt down again and took Ellie's hand. 'Hang on, Ellie. The ambulance will be here soon.'

He closed his eyes and felt himself tumbling into total blackness. The shock of it took his breath away, like plunging into cold water. *Ellie! Please, Ellie, come back to us*. Searching the darkness, he glimpsed a distant pinprick of light and slid his mind towards it. Out of the shadows of endless night, the monsters he'd always feared came creeping, invisible, terrible . . .

He fixed his eyes on the tiny point of light, now glowing blood-red and felt the wolf beside him, padding silently, keeping him safe from harm. Now he was skimming over the dew-wet grass, as fast as thought, the mists parting ahead of him and closing in behind. But the light was growing brighter, stronger, changing from red to green to an electric blue until it filled his mind.

When he opened his eyes he could see it still, or something like the memory of it. The blue light on top of the ambulance. People were talking to him, telling him to let go of Ellie's hand so they could load her on to the stretcher. 'She's going to be fine,' they said. 'Just fine.'

And he could see that her eyes were open.

Seventeen

In the school library, Mrs Utterley carefully cut out two small paragraphs from the newspaper. After some thought she opened a new file: Laxworth, Beast of. She never found anything more to put in it.

The papers might have shown more interest if there had been a decent photograph, but Dan Cornish hadn't mastered the camcorder well enough to catch the arrival of the creature, apparently out of nowhere. If he had had a stills camera ... But Frank Finnegan's pictures, clear enough of the badger-baiters and their dogs, suddenly turned lopsided and out of focus just at that point.

The men who had been there that night were shy of being interviewed but, when pressed, insisted it was just a dog they saw.

Ellie's memory of the time between the church and coming round in hospital was a total blank. 'I was saving the badgers, wasn't I?' she kept saying. 'Wasn't I? Didn't I save the badgers?' On and on until they managed to convince her there was nothing else she needed to remember. Ellie was a heroine. Stretched out on a bed of cushions on the living-room settee, she held court. She'd nearly run out of room for autographs on the plaster on her leg.

That left just Hal and the Stittles.

'Bisclavret.' Michelle rolled the name around on her tongue. 'I like that. That's a good name for him, that is.'

'Better than werewolf,' agreed Rutger. 'They gotta bad name, werewolves.'

It was several days later, after school, and they were sprawled on the rough grass under the Hanging Tree, seven of them – eight, if you counted Uncle Ho, stretched along a branch overhead, his tail swinging idly beneath him.

'It's lucky Lemmy come to us,' said Michelle. 'Most people wouldn't have realised . . .'

'They'd have locked him up,' put in Harrison.

'Given him medicines,' added Dustin.

244

'Tried to make 'im normal.'

'An' 'e's not.'

'Lemmy's special.'

'O' course our grandad, 'e knew straight off what Lemmy was.'

'He's the cunning man.'

'It used to be the cunning man that could do it. Shape-shifting.'

'Grandad ain't got the gift.'

'In the old days,' explained Michelle, 'the werewolf was the good guy, looking after the crops and the animals against the forces of evil.'

'But there's less an' less people got the gift,' said Rutger.

'That's modern life for yer,' put in Dolph.

'You gotta be someone really special to have it these days,' Rutger went on. 'Like born on Christmas Day, or something.'

'My brother was born on Christmas Day,' said Hal.

'Was he now?' said Michelle, eyes lighting up. 'You better keep an eye on 'im, then.'

'Any advice you need,' said Rutger, 'ask me grandad.'

'The cunning man?' said Hal. 'But will somebody tell me, please, what is a cunning man?' He turned to Dolph. 'You said I had the makings of a cunning man.'

Dolph nodded. 'That's what me grandad said.'

'It's sort of like a doctor,' said Michelle.

'Only better,' put in Rutger. 'It's like, there's some doctors who've got all the book-learning and they're still just doctors. Then there's the others, who've got that bit extra. They don't know themselves what it is.'

'They're the cunning men, see?' said Dolph.

'Like you sending your gran those pictures,' said Michelle. 'You knew they'd do her more good than any medicine.'

Hal tried the idea on for size. *What are you going to be when you grow up? I'm going to be a doctor.* It sounded good.

'What I don't understand,' said Hal, 'is, if it's illegal for Polly Froggett to keep badgers, why is your grandad allowed?'

'Point is,' said Michelle, 'Grandad ain't keeping them. They can come and go when they want.'

'Lemmy's building them a place to live in,' said Madonna. 'With drainpipes and chicken wire on top, so's nobody can dig 'em out, ever.'

'Lemmy keeps an eye on them.'

'An' Mia keeps an eye on Lemmy.'

'She'll keep an eye on your gran, too . . .'

While Ellie was being treated in Casualty, Hal had wandered upstairs to see Gran and found Miss Letty already there.

Gran had propped the two photographs up on the bedside cabinet. 'Thank you for those, Hal,' she said. 'Old Mr Stittle delivered them safely, as you see. We had such a long chat. About the old days. Things I'd almost forgotten came back so clearly . . .'

In the midday sunlight, the pictures had an old and faded look. They were nothing but a pale reflection of Gran. The real Gran. 'Letty's been telling me all about it, Hal. Oh, I wish I'd been there! On second thoughts, perhaps not. Leave that sort of thing to the young folks, eh? I shall have Mia to keep me out of trouble from now on.'

'Mia?' said Hal.

'Mia and Lemmy.'

It had been Miss Letty's suggestion, simple, but brilliant.

'There are the Stittles,' said Gran, 'all crammed together like sardines. And there's me, with three perfectly good spare rooms. It doesn't make sense, does it?'

So Mia and Lemmy were moving in with Gran.

'See me!' chuckled Gran. 'A lady of leisure, with living-in staff!'

'Hardly staff,' said Miss Letty. 'Since you won't be paying them. More like a commune.'

'A commune,' said Gran. 'Now there's an idea! I've still got two spare rooms . . .'

This was the old gran and no mistake. But Mia Stittle . . .!

'Mia's all right,' said Michelle equably, 'when you get to know her. She has to be bossy, 'cos she's the eldest.'

Miss Letty, as a magistrate, would see the ringleaders of the gang got the maximum sentence the law allowed.

'Six months!' said Hal. 'It's not enough!'

'No, it's not enough,' she agreed. 'But for cruelty to the dogs, they can be banned for keeping a dog for life. That should stop them, don't you think?'

She'd had a word with Mum, too, about the common. What Miss Letty said, Hal never knew, but it was OK now for him to go on the common, so long as he didn't go alone. Why would he want to go alone? He'd got friends now. *See me, friends with the Stittles!*

At school, of course, they'd still keep their distance. 'We got a reputation to keep up,' as Rutger said. But here on the common, in the real world, they were mates, with the whole summer ahead of them.

'Right!' said Rutger. 'What shall we do next?'

THE HOUSE OF BIRDS

Jenny Jones

Ominously overshadowing the village, Pelham Hall stands apart. Strange shrieks are heard from inside its walls.

Masked raiders thunder through the streets on huge black stallions. Their nightly catch is village children.

Harriet, orphaned and abandoned, sees her friends disappear, one by one.

Will she be next . . . ?

SPILLING THE MAGIC

Stephen Moore

Staying with boring relatives, life looks bleak for Billy and Mary until they find . . .

A strange book of spells.

Whisked into the mysterious, multi-coloured world of Murn they find a world on its last legs.

A world knee-deep in spilt magic.

Even with the help of flying pigs and a vege-tarian dragon, can they put the magic back where it belongs?

Another Hodder Children's book

FERAL KID

Libby Hathorn

Robbie, homeless, caught up in a crime he wants no part of . . . Iris, an old lady he mugs in a city park . . .

Their chance meeting brings about an unlikely friendship. A friendship that offers both a new future.

But can life really change for the better?

"I found this fascinating. It looks at homelessness from a different angle to *Stone Cold*, and is a great deal more optimistic, without underplaying society's indifference."

ROBERT SWINDELLS

DAUGHTER OF STORMS

Louise Cooper

Born in a supernatural storm, under a crimson sun, Shar is destined for the Sisterhood.

Innocent of the power she controls, Shar is of great value to others – who patiently lie waiting for such a soul.

But as Shar begins to realise her gift, the terror begins . . .

In a land where the gods of Order and Chaos rule – a deadly power is rising. Can Shar summon the elements to become the Dark Caller?

THE GHOST MESSENGER

Robert Swindells

Haunted by the ghosts of her grandfather and his wartime bomber crew, Meg tries to make sense of their strange and puzzling messages. These visitations disturb her sleep and her schoolwork, and are somehow intensified by the conservation work in the local woodland.

Can Meg decipher the messages before it's too late?

'This well-plotted book ... proceeds to a genuinely exciting climax.'

Junior Bookshelf

ORDER FORM

0 340 63592 4	THE HOUSE OF BIRDS *Jenny Jones*	£3.99	❏
0 340 66098 8	SPILLING THE MAGIC *Stephen Moore*	£3.99	❏
0 340 65124 5	FERAL KID *Libby Hathorn*	£3.50	❏
0 340 64070 7	DAUGHTER OF STORMS *Louise Cooper*	£3.99	❏
0 340 64672 1	THE GHOST MESSENGERS *Robert Swindells*	£3.50	❏

All Hodder Children's books are available at your local bookshop or newsagent, or can be ordered direct from the publisher. Just tick the titles you want and fill in the form below. Prices and availability subject to change without notice.

Hodder Children's Books, Cash Sales Department, Bookpoint, 39 Milton Park, Abingdon, OXON, OX14 4TD, UK. If you have a credit card you may order by telephone – (01235) 831700.

Please enclose a cheque or postal order made payable to Bookpoint Ltd to the value of the cover price and allow the following for postage and packing:
UK & BFPO – £1.00 for the first book, 50p for the second book, and 30p for each additional book ordered up to a maximum charge of £3.00.
OVERSEAS & EIRE – £2.00 for the first book, £1.00 for the second book, and 50p for each additional book.

Name..

Address...

....

....

If you would prefer to pay by credit card, please complete:
Please debit my Visa/Access/Diner's Card/American Express (delete as applicable) card no:

Signature..

Expiry Date...